Mummy for a Minute

JUDY CHRISTENBERRY

MILLS & BOON®
Pure reading pleasure

MAY 1 3 2008

First published in Great Britain 2008
Large Print edition 2008
Silhouette Books Limited, Eton House,
18-24 Paradise Road, Richmond, Surrey, TW9 1SR

© Judy Christenberry 2007

ISBN: 978 0 263 20119 2

Set in Times Roman 17½ on 23 pt.
35-0408-49185

Printed and bound in Great Britain
by Antony Rowe Ltd, Chippenham, Wiltshire

JUDY CHRISTENBERRY

has been writing romances for over fifteen years because she loves happy endings as much as her readers do. A former French teacher, Judy now devotes herself to writing full-time. She hopes readers have as much fun with her stories as she does. She spends her spare time reading, watching her favourite sports teams and keeping track of her two daughters. Judy lives in Texas. You can find out more about Judy and her books at www.judychristenberry.com

Chapter One

Damn! This wasn't going to go well. Jack Mason shifted his almost-four-year-old against his shoulder as he rang the bell at the Yellow Rose Lane fourplex.

"Ally, I need you to be really quiet and stay next to Daddy this morning, okay?"

"Okay, Daddy." Her voice didn't show any concern. She probably had no idea what he was asking, but he'd keep her out of the way. He certainly didn't want her running into The Shark's sharp bite.

The apartment door swung open and Jack

was suddenly face-to-face with the dreaded Shark. At least he thought he was. He sure hadn't expected her to open the door with a smile. "I'm looking for Miss McNabb."

Dark eyes flashed at him, darting from his face to Ally's and back again. "I'm she."

"I'm Jack Mason. Judge Robinson recommended I contact you about some cabinetry work you wanted done."

"Yes, come in, Mr. Mason and…" She paused, staring at his child.

"Um, this is my daughter, Allison. Her child-care facility closed suddenly this morning and I couldn't find a sitter. But she'll stay by my side and she won't cause any problems."

"All right," the woman said calmly, swinging the door wide, as if bringing a child to work was normal. She indicated that he should be seated, so he settled on a white couch that made him a little nervous. He perched Ally on his knee, whispering for her to be still.

"I'm not sure exactly how you work, Mr. Mason, but Judge Robinson raved about the quality of your work."

"That's very kind of him. I'd like to start by asking some questions about what you have in mind, the kind of wood, the length of time available, things like that."

"Of course." She watched him juggle the child while taking out pen and paper. "Isn't it going to be difficult to hold her and write?"

Jack glared at her. He didn't care how pretty she was. She had no business telling him how to do his job. "I'll manage."

She didn't argue with him, but her gaze remained focused on his child.

"Are we only talking about one room?" he asked.

"Yes. My third bedroom. I have a month off work and I'd like to be settled in at the end of the month."

"All right. Do you have a particular type of wood that you'd like me to use?"

"I believe you used oak in Judge Robinson's office. I liked that a lot."

"I want to draw, Daddy," Ally said, reaching for the pen.

"No, sweetheart. Daddy has to write now."

"But, Daddy—"

"No, Ally, not right now."

Ally frowned but didn't protest again. He held her a little closer.

"Do you want something similar to Judge Robinson's home office?" he asked Ms. McNabb in his best professional tone.

"Yes, I do. Except I would like more storage space."

"What kind of storage space?"

"Some bins with sliding drawers. Nothing fancy. Why don't I show you the space while we talk. That might make everything more clear." She stood, assuming he'd agree.

He had to put the pad and pen in one hand and hold Ally in the other, but he eventually was ready to follow the woman. Standing behind her, he realized she was tall. Around five foot nine, he'd guess.

To his surprise, she was wearing a polo shirt and jeans. And well-fitted, too. The denim fit like a second skin, hugging her curves. Very un-lawyer-like, he noted. Of course, his impression of lawyers was tainted by personal experience. The lawyers he'd dated in the past had been picky and difficult, always wanting to win every argument.

After going down a hall, she opened a door and walked inside. Following her, he stepped into an empty room, quite spacious for a home office.

"Very nice."

"Thank you."

"It's good that there aren't already some built-ins. That will save me the time of ripping them out."

"You have limited time?" she asked sharply.

"No, but you might. Most of my customers seem to think I can do my work overnight." He challenged her with a direct look.

"I wouldn't expect that, especially since you seem determined to hold your daughter at the same time. You did say she is your daughter, didn't you?"

"Yes, she is. I'll have child care worked out by tomorrow." Though there was no sarcasm in her voice, he was perturbed anyway.

"I see."

He began asking questions about the type of shelving she wanted. He wasn't surprised to discover she knew exactly what she had in mind. Picturing this woman in a courtroom, he saw a confident, persuasive attorney who could argue any case. Sitting Ally down on the floor with an extra pencil and a piece of paper, he began drawing the room, hoping his interpretation of her ideas would come close to what she envisioned. With a tape measure, he made sure everything would fit.

"Can we do storage bins along the back wall?" she suggested. "They could form a credenza of sorts for my desk."

He found himself in complete agreement.

The office was taking shape in the drawing, becoming a pleasant place to work. There were windows across the back wall that came about four feet from the floor. A credenza under them would be a great utilization of the space.

"Daddy, I need another sheet of paper," Ally called, distracting him.

"Okay, baby. Here you go." He ripped off another sheet of paper and handed it to his child. Then he got involved in the picture he was creating.

He asked questions of the lawyer and she provided succinct answers every time. Working for someone who knew exactly what she wanted had its advantages. And lawyers were good at that, he'd admit. It was the personal stuff they had trouble with.

An hour later, he had a finished drawing of the

room and showed it to the woman. She agreed that he'd captured exactly what she wanted.

"That's perfect. You're a wonderful artist, Mr. Mason. How long will it take to make the room look like that?"

"Three or four weeks. I can't be sure."

"Perfect. I have four weeks."

"I beg your pardon?"

"I have four weeks off work. I'll be around to monitor your work. Then, when I go back to work, I'll have my office ready."

"I don't need my work to be monitored, Miss McNabb. I'm quite capable of turning out good work without supervision." He'd clenched his teeth, knowing he was facing a battle.

"Nevertheless, Mr. Mason, I'll be here for the entire four weeks to keep an eye on the progress of your work."

"You mean you'll look at it each evening?"

"I mean I'll look at it whenever I feel like looking at it. I won't be working during those four weeks."

"Why not?" he demanded.

Affronted, she straightened, and her chin rose a notice. "That's none of your business!"

"Well, I think it is my business. It's ridiculous to take your vacation to be sure the room turns out all right. Ask Judge Robinson!"

"What I do with my time has nothing to do with you!" She put her hands on her hips, her arms akimbo, and met his eyes with a challenge. "Will you do the job or won't you?"

Jack accepted the challenge. "I'll do the job, but I won't have you peeking over my shoulder all the time!"

"Fine. When can you start?"

"Today. I'll take the measurements I need and get the lumber right away."

"Good."

She seemed prepared to stalk out of the room until a little voice asked, "Isn't my picture pretty?"

Jack felt a sense of disorientation when he looked at Ally, holding up a multicolored picture. How had she done that with the pencil he'd given her?

LAUREN LOOKED DOWN at the little girl. "Why, Ally, that's beautiful. What a nice job you did."

"Thank you. I drew a picture like Daddy, didn't I?"

"Yes, you did. Let's go put it on the refrigerator," she suggested, reaching out a hand to the child.

"No!" Jack shouted.

Lauren turned around to stare at the man. Then she realized what she'd done. She'd treated Ally like one of her brothers and sisters, pretending to be the mother, as she had ever since she was twelve.

Jack took the picture from his child. "We'll put it on our fridge at home, Ally. That's where it belongs. Uh, where did you get the markers?"

Ally tucked the box of colored markers behind her and looked at Lauren.

"I gave them to her. I thought she would enjoy using them." Lauren raised her chin again. Surely the man wouldn't object to such kindness to his child.

"She'll get the ink on herself. Ally, just use Daddy's pen, okay?"

"But, Daddy—"

"Ally, do as I say, please."

The child grudgingly took the markers from behind her back and gave them to Lauren. "Thank you," she said politely.

"You're welcome," Lauren replied.

The man took out his tape measure to begin measuring and marking down numbers on his pad of paper. He obviously hadn't realized Lauren had also given his daughter a pad of paper.

With her gaze on her father, Ally carefully moved the pad of paper behind her. A quick look at Lauren invited her silence.

Lauren just stood there, thinking how cute the little girl was. She had sandy blond hair like her father and his brown eyes, but while his features were masculine and handsome, hers were delicate and beautiful.

"Daddy, I'm hungry," the little girl said, flashing a look at Lauren.

"Yeah, baby, I'll get us some lunch in a little while," he said, obviously distracted by his work.

"I'll feed her," Lauren said quietly, hoping not to disturb him. She didn't think he'd agree to such a plan if he realized it. She held out her hand to Ally and the two left the room very quietly.

When they reached the kitchen, Lauren whispered, "Do you like grilled cheese sandwiches?"

Ally nodded, her brown eyes big.

"Good. I'll fix you one for lunch. We'll cut it into soldiers. And if you eat a soldier, you get a cookie for dessert. Okay?"

The child nodded enthusiastically. Lauren sat her at the table and began preparations for lunch. In no time, she'd made a grilled cheese sandwich and cut it into three long strips, calling each one a soldier. Then she poured her a glass of milk to go with the sandwich.

While Ally ate, Lauren made three more

sandwiches, two for Mr. Mason and one for herself. She also heated some tomato soup.

About that time, they both heard Jack's voice, calling for his daughter. He came running down the hall.

"We're in here," Lauren called. She almost broke into laughter when he burst through the open door. One would've thought he'd come slashing through the jungle to rescue the princess.

"Ally! You weren't supposed to leave my side!"

"But, Daddy—"

"I told you I was fixing her lunch," Lauren interrupted.

"I didn't hear you! And I don't need you to fix us lunch. I'll take us out to lunch. Come on, Ally."

"But, Daddy, I've almost finished my soldiers and I get a cookie for each one."

"Ally, we have to—"

"Mr. Mason, she has almost eaten all her lunch. It would be a waste of time to take her to lunch now. Besides, I've already made your lunch, too." She put a plate with two grilled cheese sandwiches and a bowl of tomato soup on the table.

He stared at the food. "I didn't ask for this!"

"No, but I thought it might save you some time."

He didn't move, staring at the food.

"Look, eat, don't eat. It makes no difference to me." She sat down to eat her own lunch.

Ally looked at Lauren's plate. "You don't have soldiers?"

"No, sweetie, only children get soldiers."

Ally leaned toward her father. "Daddy, do you want my last soldier?"

Her generosity broke through Jack Mason's stupor. "No, angel, you eat your last soldier," he told the little girl. "I have plenty of food, thanks to Miss McNabb."

He sat down at the table, saying stiffly, "I appreciate the lunch."

Lauren didn't believe him, but they ate silently and she was satisfied that he ate all the food she'd provided. Ally ate her three cookies, but she was almost half asleep by the time she finished.

"I have a bed she can sleep on," Lauren said.

"No! She stays with me." He stood and removed the corduroy jacket he was wearing and wrapped Ally in it.

Lauren watched as, carrying his child, he walked out of the kitchen toward the office.

She wasn't sure what was behind his watch-fulness, but she wanted the little girl to be comfortable. She went to the other bedroom and pushed a big chair into her future office with two pillows and a blanket to cover the child.

He had already put Ally on the floor with the jacket bunched up at one end to form a rough pillow. She patted the chair and he nodded, transferring his daughter into the chair.

"Thank you. She'll be more comfortable."

Lauren nodded and left the room. Whatever the man's hang-ups, he appeared to love his child, and that counted for something in Lauren's book.

THE PHONE RANG and Lauren answered it, pleased to hear her youngest brother's voice. "James, how are you?"

"I'm fine, sis. I, uh, thought I'd see if we were still on for dinner on Friday night?"

"Yes, of course, unless something's come up for you."

"No, I'm looking forward to it," he said.

Lauren wondered what was going on. They'd been having dinner on Friday nights ever since he'd moved out of the house and gotten his own place. He'd finished school in June and started work immediately with a software company. Next, he'd found an apartment he could afford and left home. He'd said he needed to be independent. And besides, it was time Lauren had some time to herself.

"Good," Lauren said, waiting for him to tell her the purpose of his call. Something was going on.

"Uh, what have you been doing today?"

Okay, stall tactics. "I've been interviewing

a man to turn my third bedroom into a home office. He's going to put in shelving."

"Do you need me to come check him out?"

Lauren couldn't hold back a grin. At the office, everyone would've been surprised that her brothers would think she needed their help for such a simple thing. "No, thanks, James, but I'm okay with him."

"It might be good for him to know you've got brothers who can protect you."

"I'll let him know. I have lots of pictures around the place, you know."

"Oh, yeah."

There was a prolonged silence. Lauren asked, "Is there anything in particular you want me to make for Friday night?"

"For dinner, you mean? Well, I think I'd like your chicken spaghetti. I haven't had it in a while."

"Sure. I'll be glad to make it."

"And maybe your carrot cake."

"All right."

"And, um, I thought I might bring a friend, too. Would that be all right?"

Aha! Finally they'd gotten to the point of the conversation. "Of course. I'd love to have some of your friends. Are you bringing Ronny or Doug?" she asked, keeping the smile from her voice.

"Uh, no, I thought I'd bring, uh, Cheryl."

"Who is that? A new friend?"

"Yeah. She has an apartment near me. I, uh, I'm afraid she doesn't eat enough. I thought your cooking would be good for her."

"That sounds like a good idea. I'll see you Friday evening."

Lauren hung up the phone, a smile on her lips. She'd played the role of mother for her six brothers and sisters since she was twelve. None of them had married, however. Had she done something wrong, that none of her siblings had found anyone to marry? *And what about yourself?* asked an inner voice. *Where's your special someone?*

JACK SERVED his daughter her dinner, putting macaroni and cheese on her plate, peas and carrots, and some chicken cut into tiny pieces. "There. Your dinner is ready, Ally. I expect you to eat your vegetables," he said as he helped her into her chair.

"I will, Daddy. I'm hungry."

"Good."

He sat down beside her, his plate filled with the same food. He'd learned how to cook properly when he'd found himself with a small child who needed good nutrition.

"I liked that mommy today," Ally said as she worked at scooping up the peas and carrots.

Jack had just taken a bite of his own vegetables, but her words had him spitting out food in all directions.

He hurriedly wiped his mouth and cleaned up the mess he'd made. "Uh, who are you talking about, Ally?"

"That mommy. The one who made me lunch."

"She's not a mommy."

"I know she's not *my* mommy." They had had this discussion several times over the past year. His daughter wanted to know what had happened to her mommy since everyone else at child care had a mommy. "But I think she's someone's mommy."

"No, Ally, she's not someone's mommy. She lives alone."

Ally frowned and stared at her father. "But

she cut my sandwich into soldiers, and she gave me cookies."

"Yes, she did, but she's not someone's mommy, and it's important not to call her a mommy."

"Would it make her cry?"

Jack couldn't imagine Lauren McNabb crying. She was supposed to be tough as nails. In the office, where she was known as The Shark, they would laugh at even the suggestion that she would cry about anything. "No, she wouldn't cry, but it might make her mad."

"Oh. Am I going to work with you tomorrow?"

"No, I'm calling Mrs. Smith after dinner. I think she'll keep you tomorrow."

"I want to go with you."

"No. Eat your dinner. It's almost time for your bath."

"I think she'll miss me tomorrow."

"Doesn't matter. You're going to Mrs. Smith's tomorrow. We're not having a discussion about it."

He hurriedly cleaned the dishes before he took his child to the bathroom for a quick bath. Then, looking like an angel in her nightgown, she hugged his neck and got under the covers. After she said her prayers, she whispered, "Please let me go with you tomorrow?"

"No, honey. You need to play with other children and color pictures. You'll have fun tomorrow at Mrs. Smith's."

Once he had her settled, he went to the phone. He'd tried several daycare centers before they came home, but they were all full. So he was going to call Mrs. Smith, who'd taken care of Ally when she was a baby.

"Mrs. Smith? It's Jack Mason. I've run into

a problem with child care and I wondered if you could—"

"Mr. Mason, I can't take care of children anymore. I was in a car accident and I can barely get around."

"I'm sorry to hear that. Uh, could you recommend some place where I could leave Ally?"

"No, not really. None of my friends keep children. What happened to the place you were taking her?"

"They left a child on that little bus and he died. The city shut it down."

"That's terrible. Don't take Ally back there."

"No, I won't."

"Well, sorry I can't help."

"Yeah, me, too."

Jack hung up the phone, at a loss. He had

no more ideas of what to do with Ally except take her back to work with him for one more day.

He feared Miss McNabb would be pleased.

Chapter Two

Lauren had cleaned the house twice, redone her grocery list three times and thought about redecorating her living room. What else was she supposed to do with her time?

She'd even spent some time with her neighbor across the hall last night. Sherry was a nice woman, but they had little in common other than living across the hall from each other in the fourplex on Yellow Rose Lane. Sherry had seen Jack Mason come in yesterday morning, however, and she had questions.

"Who was that hunk who came over yesterday?"

"You must mean Jack Mason. He's going to build some shelves in my new study."

"My husband wouldn't let him in the front door, looking the way he does. Good thing you're not married."

"He's a handsome man, but he's supposed to be quite talented as a carpenter."

"Yeah, but he's as handsome as sin. Of course, he brought a little girl with him. Do you take care of her?"

"No. He's going to take her to child care today."

"So it will just be the two of you? Let me know if you need company, you know, to break the sexual tension."

"Thanks, but I'm sure we'll be fine. He focuses on his work and hardly notices anything else."

"Too bad. Well, keep me up-to-date!"

Lauren had promised she would, but knew she wouldn't. There'd be nothing with which to update Sherry. Jack Mason was an attractive man, but she had no intention of getting involved with him.

His attractiveness assailed her when she opened the door to him at nine o'clock. It took a few seconds for her to realize Ally once again was in her handsome daddy's arms.

"Ally, I'm so glad you came back to see me. Come in."

After a moment, the man holding Ally said, "Do you mind if I come in, too?"

"Of course, Mr. Mason. I was expecting you."

Lauren was a little embarrassed about her reaction to the little girl. She obviously had irritated Jack with her enthusiasm, too.

"I apologize for bringing Ally again. I couldn't find anyone to take her." He stood there stiffly, not moving past the front door, as if he thought she would deny him entrance.

"Are you a mommy?" the little girl asked suddenly.

"Ally, hush," Jack Mason urged.

"Yes, sweetie, I'm a mommy," Lauren said readily. She thought of herself as a mother; after all, she'd raised her siblings after their parents' deaths.

"I'd appreciate it if you'd ignore any personal questions," Jack said hurriedly. "Ally doesn't know better."

Lauren thought about explaining her life, but then she closed her lips and said nothing. Jack Mason was her carpenter, not her lover. That established, she directed him to the office.

With Ally staring at her over her father's shoulder, Jack marched down the hall toward the empty office.

Lauren followed after a minute. He hadn't brought in any supplies. She was curious about what he was going to do.

He was coming out of her office as she got to the door and they almost collided. "Oh, sorry," she said.

"My daughter is drawing pictures and I'm bringing in supplies. If you'll excuse me," he said with exaggerated politeness.

She stood aside and waited until he was out of sight. Then she entered the office. "How are you this morning, Ally?"

"I'm fine. Daddy said I had to sit right here," she said softly.

"I know. But I have an idea." She left the room to go to her second bedroom. She'd stored a lot of things in that room that she just couldn't part with when they'd sold the family home. One of them was a small child's desk. James had used it a lot when he was little.

"Look, Ally," she said as she carried it into the office. "You can sit in the same spot but use this desk. It'll make it easier for you to draw your pictures." Lauren looked at the big smile on Ally's face. "Come on, let's try it."

"Do you think Daddy will mind?"

"I don't think so."

"Well, okay." Ally sat down in the desk. "Look! It fits me!"

"Yes, it definitely does." Lauren couldn't help but smile.

"What are you doing?" Jack demanded, pausing in the doorway, his arms full of lumber.

"I was just giving Ally a way to be comfortable. She's still in the room with you."

"Fine! Ally, stay there. I'm bringing in a lot of material and I don't want you getting hurt."

"I won't, Daddy." Before he could leave the room, she added, "But I wish I could watch *Sesame Street.*"

"Ally!" he exclaimed.

"I'm not using the television right now. I'd be glad to put on *Sesame Street.*" Lauren held her breath. Not that it really mattered to her, but she wanted Ally to be happy. Besides, *Sesame Street* was educational.

"Well, as long as you're not watching it, I guess that would be okay." He turned to his child. "Sit on the floor. I don't want you messing up that white couch."

When Lauren held out her hand, Ally took it and slid out of the desk. Together they left the office.

"You did eat breakfast this morning, didn't you, Ally?" Lauren asked after Jack went outside again.

"Daddy got me a biscuit. We were running late."

"Oh, my, I'll fix you some scrambled eggs and toast. You do like scrambled eggs, don't you?"

"I think so," Ally said, her eyes wide.

After turning on the television, Lauren hurried to the kitchen to make the child some breakfast. She'd always made sure her siblings had a good meal to start the day. Ally was just as appreciative, eating well.

After *Sesame Street* was over, Lauren invited Ally to the kitchen to make cookies. They had a great time, chatting and making chocolate-chip cookies. As Lauren had suspected, Ally's father had forgotten all about her, having gotten so engrossed in his work.

With the cookies cooling on the racks, Lauren made sandwiches for lunch.

"I think Daddy made lunch for us," Ally

said after Lauren had finished preparing the sandwiches.

"He brought lunch for both of you?"

"He bought us some sandwiches from a store."

"Ah, I see. Well, I think these sandwiches will be better. They're bacon, lettuce and tomato sandwiches. Let's go get Daddy."

When they reached the office, Jack frowned. "Is *Sesame Street* over?"

"Yes, Daddy. Lauren made us lunch."

He looked at his watch. "No. I bought us lunch, remember?"

"But I've already made bacon, lettuce and tomato sandwiches. Can't you save those for tomorrow?" Lauren waited for his answer.

"No. We'll go sit in the car and eat." Jack began putting away his tools.

"But, Daddy—" Ally began.

"You could at least eat in the kitchen so Ally will be able to eat a proper lunch."

"And, Daddy, we made cookies," Ally said as part of her plea.

"You what?" Jack asked. "I thought you were just watching *Sesame Street?*"

Lauren stepped in to protect Ally from her father's irritation. "*Sesame Street* ended hours ago. I asked Ally if she would help me make cookies. I didn't see any harm in that."

"Ally, sit in the desk and don't leave it!" Jack ordered.

"She's to sit there instead of having lunch? I think that's rather severe punishment for a small child."

"Who asked you, lady? You're not a mother. You're a lawyer! It's none of your business."

"I am too a mother! I know about—"

"You are not! You have no kids!"

"Yes, I do. I have six kids!" she yelled back, determined to win this argument.

"You're lying. Judge Robinson said you didn't have any kids."

"Well, he's wrong!"

"So where are these six kids? The oldest couldn't be more than twelve, if he's that old!"

"He's twenty-eight!" she snapped.

Jack stared at her. Finally, he said, "That's impossible."

She looked away. Her voice was lower when she explained. "My children are my brothers and sisters. My mother died when I was twelve. I became the mother. Dad hired someone to come in and do the housework once a week, but I was responsible for cooking meals and overseeing homework. I was the mother."

"My apologies. I didn't mean— Obviously,

you have the experience of being a mother. But that doesn't mean you should take over my child. She's mine, and I make the decisions."

"I'm not trying to be her mother. I'm offering to help a little. It's easy to be a mommy for a minute. Being mommy for the long haul is your job."

"Yes, it is. And we're having lunch in the car."

Lauren raised her chin. "My sandwiches are very good."

"I'm sure they are."

"They're much better than sandwiches prepared two days ago."

"You don't know when they were prepared."

"At least let Ally have her choice."

"Fine."

"Then bring your sandwiches to the table and she can choose."

They all went down the hall, Ally holding

Lauren's hand. When they went into the kitchen, Ally asked how many cookies she got if she ate all her sandwich.

"Three, just like yesterday, but I'm not cutting your sandwich into soldiers today. It would fall apart."

"Okay. Does Daddy get cookies, too?"

"If he wants them. He seems a little out of sorts."

"Daddy doesn't usually yell at me. I think he's been working too hard."

"I see. Well, I hope he feels better soon." While she talked, Lauren was serving lunch. She set a plate out for Jack, also, even though she thought he deserved to eat his prepackaged lunch.

He came into the kitchen with a brown paper bag. Taking the two sandwiches out, he stared at the sandwich already on a plate in front of him. Then he looked at his purchases. "Look, you can't keep making lunch for us."

"It's not a problem."

"Yes, it is. I'm doing a job for you, not holding my hand out for charity."

"So reduce your price. I'll make lunch for you and Ally every day and you take off the price of lunch. Maybe a whole five dollars per day."

"Fine. Five dollars a day!" With that, he sat down in the chair and picked up the warm sandwich to eat.

"Wait, Daddy! We have to say our prayer," Ally said.

"Oh, right, baby. Sorry." He bowed his head and Ally said a simple prayer.

Lauren was impressed. "That was very nice, Ally."

"Daddy taught me."

"Your daddy did a good job."

"Does that mean Daddy gets cookies, too?"

Lauren shot a look at Jack, who was stolidly chewing his sandwich, not looking at either of the females.

"Your daddy gets cookies...if he wants them."

She knew he was listening because he shot her a glance that she couldn't read. But he said nothing.

Ally leaned toward her father. "They taste good, Daddy. You'll like them."

"Thank you, baby. I'm sure I will," he muttered.

Lauren thought his words were encouraging. She ventured another suggestion. "*Mr. Rogers* starts in a few minutes. Would it be all right for Ally to stretch out on the sofa for her nap and watch that show until she falls asleep?"

"She might get the sofa dirty."

"I'll put down a sheet so she'll be comfortable. I'm afraid your hammering might make it hard for her to sleep in the office."

"Fine."

Then she passed him the plate of cookies. After hesitating, he took two.

"I think you might want more than that. The cookies are small."

He took another four. "I'll eat these while I'm working. Thank you for lunch." He stood to leave, then he thought about his daughter. "Ally, go right to sleep, okay?"

"Okay, Daddy." Her smile was big.

With an irritated look for Lauren, he strode out of the kitchen.

"I think Daddy is still mad."

"No, sweetie, he's just frustrated."

"What does that mean?"

"It means, uh, Daddy wants things to go one way but they're going the other way."

"But I think he liked the cookies," Ally said, a hopeful sound in her voice.

"Yes, I'm sure he did. Now, we've got to get you settled for your nap."

JACK TRIED to concentrate on his work, but Lauren's confession about her motherhood stayed with him. It took a lot for a person to raise her brothers and sisters.

And here he'd maligned her in his mind. He'd thought she was just being bossy, but instead she was quite experienced. As well as being beautiful. He'd noticed that at once, when she'd first opened the door. So if she was so sweet, why was she called The Shark?

Judge Robinson, who wasn't really a judge anymore, but had once been one, felt that term was one of admiration. He should know since he was the attorney in charge of the law firm. But Jack had thought it was one of disrespect.

Maybe he needed to visit with the judge. After all, Lauren seemed to be spending a lot of time with his daughter. And what was he going to do for tomorrow? Was he going to have to bring Ally with him again?

He gradually lost himself in his work. Loving the work he did was a big benefit. It made the days fly by. Then he had the evenings with Ally. She was such a sweetheart, making him feel fortunate to have his little girl.

So he was feeling good again when the door opened. He turned to see the woman from his thoughts.

He put down his tools. "Is Ally causing a problem?"

"Of course not," she told him calmly. "But I want to talk to you, please."

"About what?" he demanded.

"About Ally. You see, I don't have enough to do right now, and I thought maybe you could continue to bring your little girl and I could take care of her. It doesn't require much time, since she watches *Sesame Street* and *Mr. Rogers* and takes a nap."

"I don't think that's a good idea."

"Why? Do you have a place you can leave her?"

"No, but I'll find one."

"So why choose to leave her with strangers? Why not keep her here where you'll know what's going on?"

"I don't think a lawyer should be spending her time taking care of my child. I can't afford such expensive help."

"You'd be doing me a favor."

"Why?"

"I told you. I don't have enough to do!"

"Care to explain why you have nothing to do for four weeks, but you're not taking your vacation?"

Her cheeks turned red, drawing his attention. "I—I— Judge Robinson, the head of our firm, says I'm about to burn out and he wanted me to take some time off so it wouldn't happen. I couldn't convince him that wasn't going to happen, so he's banned me from the office for four weeks."

"And you want to entertain yourself with my child? I don't think so."

"Are you suggesting I wouldn't take good care of her? How dare you!"

"I think halfway through the four weeks, you'll find a way to work your way into Judge Robinson's good graces again and you'll abandon Ally. That'd hurt her."

"How would it hurt her any more than leaving her with a bunch of strangers? And you never said why they closed your child care center. What happened?"

"They left a child on the bus and he died," he said in a low voice. "He was five years old and he'd fallen asleep."

She stared at him. Finally, she said, "That's awful. Was Ally—"

"No. She's too young to go on field trips."

"I'm so glad." After a moment, she said, "So if you bring her here, she'll be safe."

"I don't know that."

"Yes, you do. I'll take good care of her and you can see her whenever you want."

"I don't want you to teach her things," Jack insisted.

Lauren stared at him. "You think teaching her how to make cookies will harm her?"

"No, but I won't have you teaching her to— to argue or talk back."

"You mean to act like a lawyer? Don't you think she's a little young to start her career just yet?"

"I just don't want you to fill her head with— with stuff."

"I'm not going to harm Ally in any way. I'll make sure she's happy. That's all."

"Fine," he agreed, using his favorite response.

"Fine," she replied. She left the office, closing the door behind her.

Jack stood there, his hands on his hips, staring at the space she'd occupied. This was a bad idea. He couldn't keep his distance from her if she was taking care of Ally. And he didn't want to get any closer to her.

Ever since his former girlfriend had told him she didn't want their baby and given the infant to him, he'd avoided female companionship. He didn't want Ally to become close to a woman who wouldn't stay.

Their relationship would only last four weeks. He'd have to prepare Ally for that parting. The more he thought about it, the more he thought it was a huge mistake. Maybe he should go back and tell Lauren he'd reconsidered.

He put down his tools and turned toward the door. But he hadn't taken more than a step when he stopped, changing his mind. Ally was happy. And in four weeks, he could get her in one of the schools he'd talked to. They'd have an opening then.

Picking up his drill, he began work again. But his mind remained fixed on the lawyer who wanted to take care of his child.

LAUREN STARED at the child sleeping peacefully on her sofa. She'd wanted to take care of Ally and now she could. Jack had agreed.

How strange that she'd reached out to this little girl. After raising her brothers and sisters, she'd decided she didn't want to have children. But she'd taken the first opportunity to care for this child. She thought it had something to do with her having buried the memories of raising her family. It had been difficult, with years of self-denial, especially in her teens. Dates she couldn't go on, parties she couldn't attend. But raising her siblings had also been joyful. And it was the joy that she had forgotten.

Till now.

Ally was such a sweetheart. Lauren enjoyed the child, her open and honest responses. And taking care of her would give Lauren something to focus on during her imposed hiatus.

She sat down at the kitchen table and worked out activities for Ally. She wanted the little girl to enjoy the time she spent with her. Maybe she should buy some art supplies, some books with cutouts, or storybooks.

Her excitement faded when Jack appeared in the doorway and said, "Look, I've been thinking about this and maybe it's not a good idea."

She stared at him. Then she gestured to the chair opposite her. "Let's talk about it."

"That's the last thing I want to do with a lawyer. You always think you can outtalk everyone. I'm a carpenter!"

"A carpenter who had a large business before he sold it," she pointed out. "Judge Robinson told me you were a major player in the real estate market here in Dallas, so don't play the innocent with me!"

"I'm not trying to mislead you. You're

known for your ability to argue your case. But I'm talking about my daughter. She's not open for discussion."

"Why?"

His eyebrows soared. "Because I have the final say about my child. And I think, one-on-one, you're going to get too close to her. She'll think— She's going to see you as— I don't want to risk it."

"She'll see me as what?"

"Damn it, she'll see you as a mother. As *her* possible mother!"

"I'm sure she won't. All I'm offering is to take care of her for four weeks, while you make my office for me. I don't see that as a problem."

"You may not, but I do! So, I'll find a place for her to go to school. That's all."

She continued to plead her case. "What if you don't?"

"I will. Don't concern yourself."

"Of course I'm concerned! And there's no need to enlist a group of strangers to take care of Ally when I'm right here and willing to care for her."

He held his ground. "I'll find a place for her."

"But she likes it here!"

His voice rose as his patience unraveled. "I don't care!"

"But—"

"Daddy? Why are you yelling at Lolly?" Ally asked from the doorway.

Chapter Three

Jack turned to stare at his daughter. "Who the hell— I mean, who is Lolly, sweetheart?"

Lauren cleared her throat. "My little brother used to call me that because it's easier to say than Lauren. It's about the only *L* word children learn quickly. I told Ally she could call me Lolly."

Jack glared at her. "I guess that's better than calling you— Never mind. I still don't think her staying here is a good idea."

"Suppose we try it for a few days. If it's not working out, you can find another place."

And suddenly Jack could no longer argue.

He didn't have the stamina. Maybe that was why they called her The Shark. The woman was relentless. "I'm going to keep looking. When I find a place, I'm putting her in it. So be prepared."

He spun around to leave and found himself facing his daughter. "Sweetheart, you're going to stay with—with Lolly until I can find a place for you to go to school."

Ally's face broke into a big smile. "I like that."

Muttering about women, Jack stalked down the hall.

LAUREN'S SMILE matched Ally's. "I hope you're happy staying here, Ally. I am."

"I love it, Lolly. Maybe Daddy won't ever be able to find a place for me!"

"Well, it will only be for four weeks, sweetheart. Then I'll have to go back to work."

"Where do you work?"

"Downtown. Maybe I can take you down there one day, and we could have lunch."

"Will Daddy go with us?"

"No. He'll be working here. But we'd be back before he finished work. We'll talk to him about it."

That was one conversation she dreaded.

THE WEEK PROGRESSED quietly. Lauren did her grocery shopping and made her trip to the art supply store at night, not testing Jack's patience about taking Ally out in the car.

On Friday, her day was spent in the kitchen, with Ally beside her, supposedly helping, getting ready for dinner that night.

"Who is coming?" Ally asked again.

"My baby brother, the one who used to use the desk."

"Is he my age?"

"No, he's almost twenty-two."

Ally's eyes got large. "That's lots older, isn't it?"

"Yes. He lives in his own apartment, and he's bringing a friend who lives there, too."

"Aren't you making a lot of food?"

"Yes, I decided I'd freeze some for later."

Ally gave her a confused look.

"You know, like ice cream. It stays good until you thaw it out."

"Oh."

It was just before noon when Lauren finally slid two large casserole dishes into the oven. "Now we need to fix lunch. Your daddy will be hungry."

"Me, too."

Lauren made roast beef sandwiches and sent Ally to call her father. The child came running back down the hall.

"Daddy said in a little while."

Lauren took Ally's hand and went back down the hall. As she suspected, Jack was working away, with no knowledge that he'd said no to lunch.

"Jack?"

"Uh-huh?"

"I want you to come to lunch. It's all ready."

"Just a minute," he muttered.

"Do you need some help?"

"Yeah, can you come hold this in place while I nail it?" he asked, still focused on his work.

Lauren did as he asked. She didn't realize quite how close she would have to get to him. But as she held the wood, his arms went completely around her to nail it in place. His rock-hard chest pressed against her, leaving her no avenue of escape.

She couldn't help wonder what it would be

like to have his arms around her for real, pulling her into a kiss.

"Okay, now we can go."

His words cut into her heated reverie. "Go where?"

"To lunch. You said it's ready now."

"Right." That was why she'd come into the office in the first place. Somehow she'd gotten sidetracked.

Ally took his hand. "I'll show you, Daddy. Lolly's been cooking all morning."

He looked at Lauren. "We don't need anything complicated for lunch."

"No, I've been cooking for this evening. My brother and his friend are coming over for dinner."

He stared at her. "You can cook?"

"Of course I can. My mother taught me a lot of recipes before she died, and I've learned others. Did you think I ate out every evening?"

"I know professional women who do that."

They had reached the kitchen and the aroma of roast beef lingered in the air. He noticed it at once, his gaze going to the plate on the table. "We're having roast beef?"

"Yes, is that a problem?"

"Not at all. I love roast beef."

"Good. Ally thought you did."

She finished pouring glasses of iced tea for the two adults and milk for Ally. "Okay, Ally, you can say the prayer for us."

The child did so and then beamed at her father. "It's a good lunch, isn't it, Daddy?"

"You bet, honey," he agreed after taking his first bite. "It's wonderful. I think I may owe more than five dollars for this one."

"It'll average out. Besides, I froze a lot of it."

"Like ice cream, Daddy."

"Yeah, I do that, too. Some days, I don't feel like cooking, but Ally needs a good meal."

"Yes, she does."

"Lolly made something else with chicken in it," Ally said, frowning as she tried to remember what it was.

"Chicken spaghetti, sweetie." She looked at Jack. "It's my brother's favorite."

"I've never heard of that."

"It's a casserole that my mother made. All the kids love it."

"Ah. Down home food."

"Yes. When one of them asks for that, I know something's up."

"So what's up tonight?"

"The friend is female. He says she doesn't eat enough and he wants me to feed her. I think he wants me to meet her, but he doesn't want to say it's something important."

"How old is he?"

"Almost twenty-two. He's the baby."

"Have any of your other brothers and sisters married?"

"No, none of them."

"You know, at twenty-two I fell in and out of love every other month. I wouldn't attach too much to this visit."

"Maybe. But James makes good decisions."

"Are any of your other siblings coming this evening?"

"No, just James. One brother, Steve, is in the army and doing his training. The two oldest, Bill and Barry, don't expect me to cook for them anymore. My sisters are twins, twenty-five. Regina works for a dress designer. We call her Reggie. And her twin Virginia, who we call Ginny, is working on her master's in history, hoping to go on for her doctorate."

"If she can afford that, she's doing well."

"She works as a waitress to supplement her share of the insurance money."

Jack just shrugged his shoulders. "That's not easy. I know what it's like to have two jobs." He nodded at Ally. "Speaking of which, I'd better get back to the paying one." Thanking her for lunch, he went back down the hall to work.

After Lauren put Ally down for her nap, she set the table for dinner for three, wanting everything perfect. She'd even bought fresh flowers the night before for a centerpiece. Now she did the arrangement and put it in the middle of the table.

She chose some soft music on the stereo to play during dinner. Just as she was moving away, they broke into the music for a weather alert. Bad weather was moving into the metro area that evening. Possible thunderstorms, even the threat of a tornado.

It was late fall in Dallas. They frequently had tornado alerts, but they seldom materialized. And they could use some rain. They hadn't had much this fall.

Lauren shrugged her shoulders. Not much she could do about it.

She thought of something she'd been planning to do some research on. Now would be a good time while Ally was sleeping. She moved into her bedroom, where her law books were stored temporarily. She got lost in her work, much as Jack did in his, not thinking of Ally until she heard her tiny whisper.

"Lolly?"

"Oh, sorry, baby, is it time for you to be up?"

"I think so. It's very dark outside. Did Daddy go home without me?"

Lauren looked out her bedroom window, surprised to see dark clouds. She checked her watch. It was four-thirty, later than Ally usually slept, but it shouldn't be totally dark outside.

She hurried to the television and turned it to the Weather Channel. They were predicting a big storm at any moment, with possible tornadic activity. Lauren wasn't sure what to do.

Deciding not to bother Jack, since there was nothing he could do, she found a game Ally could play and used it to distract her.

"I love chutes and ladders," Ally exclaimed as they played a second game.

"Yes, it's fun, isn't it? Does Daddy play it with you?"

"Sometimes. But I have to take my bath and get in bed. So we play it on Saturdays."

"I see."

"Can we go see if Daddy wants to play now?"

"Well, he's working. But it's almost time for him to stop. Maybe we'd better go tell him about the storm."

About that time, the rain began. It was thundering down hard, and she wasn't surprised to see Jack at the windows, staring out.

"We came to tell you about the storm," Lauren announced from the door.

"Yeah, I've noticed. It's coming down pretty hard."

"Yes."

"When are your dinner guests arriving?"

"At six. I think I need to go put the casserole in the oven to heat up in case the electricity goes out."

"Does that happen much here?"

"I don't know. I just moved in a month ago.

We sold the family home and divided up the money between the seven of us. I bought this place then. The owner was selling each unit by itself. I was lucky and got the owner's place."

"Go on and put it in the oven. Ally can help me pack up."

"You can't leave in this downpour. You'll need to wait the storm out here. It's too dangerous to drive in it."

"We don't want to get in your way. We'll be fine."

"That makes no sense. You'll probably be doing me a favor. I'll have a lot of food prepared and they probably won't come."

She went to the kitchen to start heating the casserole. Then she looked for candles. Just in case.

She put the candles where she could easily find them.

Just then, the doorbell rang. It was five-fifteen, too early for her guests. She hurried to the door and swung it open. Bill and Barry were standing on the front porch. "Hi. What are you two doing here?"

"We wanted to make sure you were doing okay in your new place. With a storm like this, you might have problems," Barry said as he moved inside.

"But you shouldn't have driven in this storm," Lauren protested.

"We didn't think it would get this bad," Bill confessed. "If we hadn't been over halfway here, we would've gone back."

"Come on in and dry off. There are some towels in the bathroom."

She went to her bedroom and found some sleep shirts her brothers could wear. "These aren't good-looking, like your shirts, but they are dry."

About that time, Jack and Ally came down the hall. "Oh, Jack, these are my brothers, Bill and Barry. They came to check up on me. This is Jack Mason. He's working on my office."

They all shook hands. Then the guys asked to see what Jack had done so far in the room.

"You might as well show them, Jack. You can't possibly take Ally out in this."

As they went past the dining room, the guys noticed the dinner table set for three. "You two were invited to dinner?" Barry asked.

"No, I think your brother James and a friend were having dinner with Lauren," Jack said evenly, showing no resentment at Barry's tone.

"Are they still doing that?" Bill asked. "I

thought he would've gotten over that after a few weeks."

"I believe he's bringing someone to meet your sister."

"A girl? Is he bringing a girl? What's wrong with the boy?" Barry demanded. "You don't do that unless you're planning on doing something permanent. He's not even twenty-two yet. Has he lost his mind?"

By that time, they'd reached the office and Jack showed them his drawing of what the room should look like when he'd finished.

"Hey, this will be nice," Bill exclaimed.

Before anything else could be said, they all heard the doorbell ring again.

"Damn, he shouldn't be bringing a girl here," Barry protested again.

"Maybe we should wait a minute and give Lauren a chance to meet her without any protests from you two," Jack said with a grin. "It might make it hard on James."

"You know James?" Bill asked.

"No, Lauren told me about him at lunch."

"You ate lunch with Lauren?"

"She insists on making lunch every day for us. I'm deducting a certain amount from my bill. She's also taking care of Ally, too, until I can find someone to take her."

"Cute kid, but did Lauren volunteer for that? I mean, she works long hours. I don't see—"

"You didn't know she's not working for four weeks?"

The two men stared at Jack, their mouths open. Then they whirled around as one and started back to the front of the house.

"Uh-oh. Looks like I spilled the beans. We'd better go apologize to Lauren," he muttered, taking Ally's hand.

"I didn't see any beans, Daddy."

"I know, honey, but I should've."

They reached the kitchen just as the two older brothers were greeting the other two guests. Lauren introduced Jack and Ally to James and a beautiful young woman named Cheryl.

Before Jack could say anything, Barry demanded to know why his sister wasn't working for four weeks. Lauren shot Jack a look, obviously understanding how that information had gotten out.

"I'm taking some time off. Why? Is that a problem?"

All three brothers stared at her. Finally, Bill said, "No, not if that's what you want to do."

"Yes, it is. I'm getting settled in my new place. And I'm taking care of Ally while Jack works."

"Oh, sure. We didn't realize Jack was a friend." Bill shot a look at Jack, obviously reevaluating his status as friend—or maybe more than friend.

Jack looked at Lauren, but he said nothing.

"Yes, well, I'll need to add a few places to the table," Lauren said, not bothering to explain, as she had to Jack earlier that day.

"May I help?" Cheryl asked, and Lauren immediately gave her something to do, making her feel welcome.

Within minutes, Lauren had expanded her dinner for three to dinner for seven. She added more broccoli to the pot and cut up more salad. She put Bill and Barry to peeling more potatoes, and suggested to James that he entertain Jack and Ally.

Just as they sat down to dinner the electricity went out. Lauren found the candles and matches and they ate their dinner by candlelight. Outside, the storm raged.

"I like this dinner, Lauren. What did you call the casserole?" Jack asked.

"Chicken spaghetti. It was one of Mom's favorites."

"Yeah, I love it," James said, smiling at Cheryl.

"I'd love the recipe," Cheryl said softly, looking at Lauren.

"Of course. Mom got it out of a church cookbook, so it didn't originate with her. But it's very filling and has a lot of good things in it," Lauren explained.

"It's a good thing you fixed a lot of it," James said, "since Bill and Barry arrived."

"You think we shouldn't check on Lauren?" Barry demanded.

"You know I always come on Friday," James pointed out.

"Yeah, but this is a bad storm. We were

afraid she might find she had a leak or something like that," Bill said. "You never know in a new place until it's tested."

A crack of thunder emphasized his words.

"Ooh, that was close," Lauren said, staring out the window.

Ally whimpered, and her father comforted her. "We're okay, baby. Don't worry."

Cheryl said, "I haven't seen a storm like this before."

"I remember a bad one when we were little," Bill said. "We were frightened, but Mom and Dad calmed us down."

"Yes, they were good at that," Lauren said. "It's different when you're the adult. It's easier to convince a child."

"Yeah," James agreed. "You used to tell me everything was all right."

"But I was right, wasn't I?" Lauren asked.

"Yeah, but—" Just then a booming crack of thunder resounded. "Do you want to tell me again?"

"I don't think it works as well when you're an adult."

Lauren almost ducked at another loud boom of thunder. "Maybe we should just pretend it isn't storming."

Jack gave her a skeptical look.

She squared her jaw and got up from the table. "How about dessert? I made carrot cake."

Her brothers showed enthusiasm, but Cheryl and Jack looked a little unsure.

James leaned over to Cheryl. "You'll love it, honey. It's one of Lauren's specialties."

"I'm willing to try it, but I've never had it before." Cheryl gave Lauren a smile.

"Don't worry. I won't be upset if you don't

like it. James, will you get some saucers, and Bill, some clean forks, please?"

She took one of the candles from the table into the kitchen. The cake was heavy and she realized she couldn't carry it and the candle at the same time. "Barry? I need some help here."

She heard footsteps and assumed Barry had come to assist her. "Thanks. The cake is too heavy and—"

Turning around, she almost dropped the cake when she realized it was Jack who had followed her to the kitchen. "What happened to Barry?"

"He was still eating chicken so I volunteered. You needed help?"

Help was just what she needed. Help from her brother, not Jack. Somehow just being alone with him in the kitchen was making her nervous. She could feel her heart pick up the pace, and her voice was breathless when she finally responded, "You can take the cake."

Jack reached out for it and, underestimating the heft, nearly dropped it. Acting on instinct, she flung out her arms and they met his hands as he got a tighter grip on the plate.

From the mere contact she felt a sizzle course from her hands up her arms, jolting her with its intensity. Pulling back as if burned, she grabbed the candle and spun toward the door, trying not to let Jack know she was running away.

The quick motion extinguished the flame on the candle, plunging the kitchen into darkness.

In her haste to escape, she ran into something hard, warm and...all male.

Chapter Four

Shivering from the contact, Lauren took a step back. "S-sorry," she muttered.

"I'll move out of your way," Jack said.

"Th-thank you." She really had to stop stammering. Good thing it was too dark for him to see the blush on her face.

Once she was sure Jack was not in her way, she turned on a burner on the stove and lit the candle. Then she led the way back to the dining room. Even after they reached the table, she still didn't look Jack in the eyes.

"I thought you were going to help me, Barry," she said pointedly.

"I was still eating and Jack volunteered. I figured you'd like him better in the dark than you would me." He grinned at his sister.

Lauren stared at Barry. What could he mean? Then she remembered them asking earlier about why she wasn't working—and their decision that Jack was a friend.

She debated explaining the situation, but she didn't want to tell them that her boss had sent her away from the office. They might think her job was in danger. No, she'd just have to get through the rest of the evening without any repercussions.

The carrot cake was a big success, and the storm began to ease, though it didn't completely go away. But it calmed down enough that everyone relaxed.

"Hey, we're going to the Rangers game tomorrow night," Bill said. "If anyone wants to go, we can turn in the tickets we got and get more so we can all sit together. How about it, Jack? Do you like baseball?"

"Yeah, I do, but I have Ally. I don't think—"

"You and Lauren can handle one kid between you, can't you? Because I know Lauren likes the Rangers."

"You do?" Jack asked in surprise.

"Yes, I do," she said, determined to show that he didn't know anything about lawyers.

"Great! I'll get four tickets, unless you want to make it six tickets, little brother." Bill looked expectantly at James.

"Yeah, make it six. I don't want to miss out on a family gathering."

"I think Ally will need a ticket, Bill," Jack said. "If you're sure you don't mind if we tag along."

"No, it'll be great fun." Bill stood. "Well,

we'll help with the dishes and then get out of here. We've outstayed our welcome tonight."

Lauren shook her head. "You don't have to help with the dishes, Bill. I'll get them after the lights come on."

"Naw, sis, after that great meal, the least we can do is help with the cleanup." He stood and began stacking the dishes and Barry did the same. James told Cheryl to keep Ally company and began helping, too. Jack joined in, carrying dishes to the kitchen.

When everything was straightened, they all moved toward the front door.

"We'll meet here tomorrow night at five-thirty, okay?" Bill asked.

Everyone agreed. Jack put Ally on his shoulders as she snuggled against him.

Lauren watched all her guests leave together, not giving her any opportunity to talk alone to

Jack. She'd hoped for a chance to explain what was going on with her brothers.

But going to a baseball game in a group wouldn't make a difference. Would it?

LAUREN WAS READY at five o'clock in case Jack got there early. Unfortunately, her two oldest brothers got there first, followed by James and Cheryl. Jack and Ally got there just five minutes before it was time to go.

"Come on, Jack. We can all squeeze into Bill's van," Barry called.

"Ally, do you need to go to the bathroom before we go?" Lauren asked softly.

"Yes, please," Ally agreed and turned loose of her father's hand.

Lauren took her inside her apartment. While there, she asked Ally if she was excited about going to the game.

"Yes, but what is the game?" Ally asked.

"Baseball. It's where they throw the ball and try to hit it with a bat."

"Okay. Daddy said it was fun."

"Good. I hope you like it. And you get to eat a hot dog at the ball game."

Ally stared at her. "I have to eat a dog? But I like dogs."

"No, honey, not a dog. A hot dog is a wiener in a bun. You'll like it."

"Okay. Do they have ice cream?"

"They do. After you eat your hot dog, you'll get some ice cream. If your daddy doesn't buy you any, I will."

Together they went outside to find everyone else in the van. Jack was in the backseat, waiting for the two of them. They managed to squeeze in beside him where Lauren carefully and deliberately put Ally between her and Jack.

An hour later, they were parked and walking to the stadium.

"Hurry, guys, they're playing the national anthem already," Bill called.

Jack scooped up Ally and put her on his shoulders. "This should speed things up a little," he said with a grin.

"Good thinking," James said. "If you need me to spell you, just let me know."

"Thanks, but she's a lightweight."

Lauren walked beside Jack because the others were paired off, also. But she was feeling a little odd. The four others thought she and Jack were a couple. She only hoped Jack didn't realize what they thought.

JACK HOPED Lauren didn't realize he'd taken advantage of her brothers' misunderstanding their relationship. But he hadn't been to a baseball game in three years. The opportunity to go tonight had been too tempting to refuse.

He felt excitement rising as they approached the stadium and the crowds of fans milling about. His little girl tugged on her daddy's ear.

"Daddy? Daddy? Where is the hot dog I have to eat, so I can have ice cream?"

"Who said you had to eat a hot dog?"

"Lolly. She promised."

Jack turned to look at Lauren. "You promised her ice cream if she ate a hot dog?"

"I thought she should have something solid before she ate ice cream."

"Okay. Then let's get our hot dogs."

"Why don't I get the hot dogs and you go ahead and find our seats." She turned to Bill. "Give me my ticket so I can stop and get the hot dogs before I go sit down."

"Sure, here you go. Barry, you stay with sis

and get us some hot dogs. James, you want them to get you some, too?"

Soon, only Barry and Lauren were left at the concession with orders from everyone. They needed two trays to carry it all to the seats.

"Hey, Bill got us great seats," Barry said.

"Yes, he did, didn't he?" Lauren agreed. But she noted the empty seat beside Jack, and she knew it was saved for her. She sat down beside him as they passed around the food.

"Thanks for getting everything," he said. "Now we're all set for the beginning of the game."

During the first few innings, the game was so exciting, Jack hoped Lauren forgot about the fact that they appeared to be together. Her brothers seemed to forget as they cheered the Rangers on. But after getting a four-run lead, the Rangers seemed to settle for strikeouts.

Ally, having had her ice cream, grew sleepy. Lauren held out her arms to the child and she crawled into Lauren's lap.

"You don't have to hold her," Jack protested.

"No, I'm happy to hold her. Enjoy the game."

He figured his child would demand his attention in a few minutes, so he watched the game, waiting. But Ally never asked for him take her. She seemed perfectly content in Lauren's arms.

Jack watched Lauren out of the corner of his eye. She didn't appear tired of Ally. Finally, he said, "I think I should take her now."

"Wait until we're ready to go. You can take her then."

"Aren't you tired? I imagine your back is hurting."

"No, we're fine. There's only one more inning."

When the game ended, he held out his arms

for his little girl. Lauren transferred her warm body over to her father. Ally whimpered at having her sleep disturbed, but she immediately settled down in her father's arms and went right back to sleep.

"I don't think she even woke up," Lauren whispered to him.

"She sleeps soundly," he agreed.

When they reached Lauren's apartment, she told everyone goodbye and went inside. She noticed her brothers gave her strange looks, but she wasn't going to pretend to say a special good-night to Jack and Ally.

Tomorrow she'd call her brothers and tell them the truth…even if it did embarrass her.

Since it was Sunday, she knew Jack and Ally wouldn't be coming. She had the entire day to herself. After church, she cleaned house, did some laundry, and watched television. And missed Ally.

What had Jack done with his Sunday? Did he take Ally to Sunday school? Did he spend the afternoon playing games with his child?

She tried to call both Bill and Barry, but neither was home. She'd have to remember to call them later. It was clear that they thought her relationship with Jack was different than the reality. Jack wanted nothing to do with a lawyer. And definitely not with a woman. He seemed awfully protective of Ally's emotions.

As he should be.

But she wasn't a threat. Being a mother was not high on her list of things to do. Been there, done that. But Ally was sweet and deserved the best.

She was getting ready for bed when Reggie, one of the twins, called her.

"Hi, Reggie. How are you doing?"

"I'm doing fine, but I hear you're doing better."

"What are you talking about?"

"Barry called and told me all about your new guy. He sounds terrific."

"My new— Oh. He's—he's just a friend, that's all."

"That's not what Barry says. He thinks you're pretty serious about him. Why haven't you told us about him before?"

"Reggie, I promise there's nothing serious going on. I would've invited everyone over to meet him if we were serious."

"Hmmm, okay, I'll be waiting for my invitation. I've got to go, but keep me informed."

Lauren hung up the phone and muttered, "Thanks, Barry."

Of course, she should've told Reggie that

Jack was simply working for her. But somehow it had seemed easier to say he was a friend. It wasn't the truth, but it would do for now. After her office was finished, she'd tell them all that they had drifted apart.

Yes, that would work.

If Barry kept his mouth shut and didn't say anything to Jack.

She hoped it would work out. Otherwise, Jack would think she was an old maid looking for a man to trap. And she'd be horribly embarrassed.

But as she crawled into bed, she couldn't help thinking about the fact that Jack and Ally would be back in the morning. It was Ally she missed, of course. Not Jack.

No, not Jack.

JACK BOTH DREADED and looked forward to going to work on Monday morning. He felt he'd taken advantage of Lauren's brothers by accepting the invitation to the ball game. But he'd had a great time, and Ally had enjoyed it, too, mainly because of the ice cream and the mascot dressed up like a horse. But whatever the reason, she didn't suffer.

He wondered, though, if Lauren was angry with him. Should he apologize?

He decided to play it by ear. If she fired him, he'd definitely know he'd made a mistake. But maybe they could return to their former roles, employer-employee, and not discuss the weekend.

"I missed Lolly yesterday," Ally said as they drove to Lauren's apartment.

"It wasn't a workday, baby. You'll see her today," he reminded his child.

"I'm glad. I bet she missed me, too."

"Mmm-hmm." He didn't want to agree with

her, but he couldn't come right out and say Lauren probably was grateful for a day off.

He rapped on Lauren's front door, a little anxiety building as she took a long time to answer.

"Sorry if I kept you waiting. Hello, Ally. How are you this morning?" she asked even as the little girl threw herself into waiting arms.

"I missed you!" Ally announced.

"Me, too. Come on. I'll fix you some breakfast."

Jack stood there in shock as his child went, hand-in-hand with Lauren, to the kitchen.

"Hey! She had breakfast," he shouted.

Lauren turned around to stare at him. "What did she have?"

Jack dropped his head. "Something from a drive-through. But she's not hungry. Right, Ally?"

"I like Lauren's breakfast better, Daddy," Ally, the traitor, announced.

The two females continued on their way, leaving Jack speechless. Ally had never complained before. It was Lauren's fault, he decided.

Women! He'd known better than to let Ally be around one of them. Lauren acted like she was Ally's mother. She wasn't. Nor was she likely to be. He just hoped Ally wouldn't be too terribly hurt when they left this job.

He walked to the back of the apartment, ignoring what was going on in the kitchen. His stomach growled, but he refused to think about scrambled eggs. Or anything else the woman fixed.

When Lauren appeared in the doorway of the study with a plate in her hands, he stared at her. "What?"

"Your daughter was concerned that you hadn't had a proper breakfast. So here it is."

She set a plate with scrambled eggs, bacon and toast on a nearby chair and left the room.

Jack tried to ignore the food, but he finally gave up, took the plate and ate the delicious breakfast. He'd almost finished when Lauren reappeared with a cup of steaming coffee.

"Sorry, but it took time for the coffee to brew."

"Thanks. I enjoyed the food, but it's not necessary for you to cook breakfast for either of us. You're already making lunch."

She shrugged her shoulders and said nothing. Then, as he sipped the fragrant coffee, she said, "There's a full pot if you want refills."

He immediately vowed not to ask for a refill. But it was great coffee.

"I need to go grocery shopping. Is it okay if Ally goes with me?"

"No! No, she can stay here with me."

"I know she can, but it would break up her day, make it more interesting. I'll put her car seat in my car. She'll be perfectly safe."

"But she'll think— No, I don't want her to miss *Sesame Street.*"

"I was going to wait until it was over."

That left him with no excuse to keep Ally there with him. "Okay, but just this once. I don't want her to get used to going places with you."

Lauren glared at him as if he'd insulted her. "I told you she'll be safe."

"Yeah, I know."

LAUREN HADN'T GONE grocery shopping during the day in years. When she and Ally got to the store, they discovered a lot of mothers, with their small children hanging on to the carts. Ally actually saw another little girl who had gone to her nursery.

"I know her," Ally said, pointing at the child.

"You do? Where do you know her from?"

"She went to my school."

"Oh. Well, I think you should say hello to her." She pushed the cart closer to the other woman and her child. "Hello. Ally says she went to school with your little girl."

The two children acknowledged each other shyly. The mother looked at Lauren.

"I don't remember seeing you picking Ally up."

"No, her father did that. But I wanted to ask if you've found another school for your little girl. Jack has looked, but he hasn't found any openings."

"Actually, I have. But not until next week. The Tiny Tots Care School has an opening for

Lila. I think they may have room for another student. You see, they've had several families move away this week."

"Oh, that's good news. I think Ally needs the training they provide and the socialization, too."

"I agree, and it will be nice for Lila to have a friend in the class."

"Yes, for Ally, too. Thanks a lot. We'll call them right away." With a friendly nod, Lauren pushed her basket down the aisle.

They had gone down a second aisle before Ally spoke.

"You don't want me to come to your house anymore?"

Lauren looked at the sad expression on the child's face. "Why would you think that, Ally?"

"Because you said I should go to school."

"Oh, sweetheart, I want you to go to school

to learn, not because I don't want you at my house. And I can pick you up after school, feed you lunch and you can take your nap at my house…until Daddy finishes his work."

"What happens then?"

"You'll go to school, all day, I guess. I mean, I have to go back to work. And your daddy will go to another job."

Ally gave her such a sad look. Lauren suddenly realized why Jack was being so careful about her relationship with Ally. She was going to hurt her.

They remained silent the rest of the shopping trip until their groceries were stored in the car and they began the drive home.

"Ally, I've enjoyed spending time with you, and when your daddy finishes the job, I won't see you all the time. But I can see you on weekends. We can have a playdate on

Saturday. What do you and your daddy do on Saturdays?"

"We run errands and sometimes play games."

"Well, you and I could do something while your daddy runs errands. Wouldn't that be fun?"

Ally nodded her head. Then she said, "Are you going to tell Daddy about the school?"

"Not yet. We—we'll wait a while. When we have to tell him, we will. But until then, we'll enjoy ourselves," Lauren said. She was enjoying spending time with Ally and she wasn't ready to give her up.

Chapter Five

Jack found himself listening for Lauren and Ally's return from grocery shopping. Only because of his concern for Ally, he assured himself. He didn't like Lauren taking Ally anyplace. She was acting as if Ally was her child.

Ally would have a hard time when the job ended and she had to go back to school. And he hadn't found a school yet willing to take her.

He was facing that challenge when he heard them coming in. He put down his tools and went to the kitchen. Lauren was telling Ally to stay while she went out to the car and got the other bags of groceries.

"I'll get the groceries," he said. "You two can start putting things away."

He didn't wait for an answer. Her car was parked right next to the entrance and he grabbed two bags and carried them in. Setting them down, he turned and went out again. When he returned with the last two bags, Lauren was putting the groceries away.

"Thank you. It wasn't necessary," she said, not looking at him.

"Daddy is strong," Ally said, smiling at her father.

"Thanks, baby. But you and I never buy that many groceries."

"Lolly cooks lots, Daddy. But we get carrot cake for lunch today. Lolly said."

"That's very nice. Don't get in her way, okay? If you want, you can come back here with me and draw some pictures."

"No, I want to stay with Lolly."

There was a sadness on Ally's face that bothered Jack. "If you're sure."

He waited until she nodded. Then he said, "I'd better get back to work."

Lauren said nothing, not even acknowledging his presence. He turned and left the room, feeling a little sad himself, though he couldn't say why.

Once he got back to work, his mood improved. Until Lauren called him to lunch. Today they were having thick ham-and-cheese sandwiches. They were delicious, which reminded him again of the deal he'd made with her. It had been a mistake, but it seemed stupid to refuse lunch now.

After the sandwiches, she cut them generous pieces of the carrot cake.

"This cake is terrific, Lauren," he finally said.

"Thank you. If you'd like, I'll send you home with some for dessert this evening. I certainly can't eat all of it."

"No, we don't need dessert that often."

"All right, but it's going to go to waste, just sitting here."

"We'll still be able to eat it tomorrow."

"Yes, of course."

Ally, eating her own piece of cake, said, "I like Lolly's cake."

"So do I," Jack hurriedly said. "But too much cake isn't a good thing."

"Why?" Ally asked.

"Because too much sugar isn't good for you."

After an awkward silence, Lauren concurred, "Daddy's right. You need to eat a balanced diet. Not too much of any one thing."

"It would be like only eating ice cream. It's good, but it won't make you grow."

"But I like ice cream!" Ally protested.

"That's exactly your daddy's point. We have to eat other things as well as ice cream, like your sandwich." Lauren smiled at her.

Jack found himself wishing she'd give him a smile like that.

What? Where did that come from? He jumped up from his seat. He was spending way too much time with her over lunch. He needed to get back to work.

As he excused himself and hurried back to the office, he noticed Lauren's scent seemed to follow him. Like tendrils, the sweet floral aroma seemed to wrap itself around him, embracing him.

Or maybe he was just imagining it.

JACK WAS PACKING UP his tools when he heard a male voice coming from the front of the apartment. He found that disturbing until he realized it was Bill's voice.

Much to his surprise, Bill came back to the office to look at the work he'd done so far. "Nice job," he commented as he studied the shelves Jack had already put in.

"Thanks," Jack said.

"Hey, I came to see if you play poker. We're having our monthly poker party. It's penny ante, no one wins more than ten dollars all night. But we're short a guy. I thought maybe you could join us."

He hadn't played poker in years. Not since Ally was born.

"That would be fun, but Ally—"

"I asked Lauren. She said she'd take care of Ally."

Jack stared at the other man. "I-I'll have to talk to Lauren. I don't want to ruin her evening."

"Okay. We'll go ask her together. But those two seem to get along really well. Good deal, huh?" he said, winking.

Jack pretended not to understand and kept walking to the kitchen where Ally usually went after her nap. When he entered the kitchen, he found it empty. Turning around, he looked at Bill.

"They were in the living room when I came in," Bill said cheerfully.

Jack wondered why the man couldn't have said something. He headed for the living room, wishing Bill wasn't right behind him. He would've preferred to talk to Lauren alone.

"Lauren? Uh, Bill said you agreed to keep Ally for me this evening. It's not necessary that I go, so—"

"I don't mind. I thought the two of us

would go to see that new Disney movie. Ally wants to see it. Then I'll bring her back here and put her to bed. She can even spend the night, if you want."

"No, I'll pick her up. I promise I won't be late." He paused, then tried once more. "But there's no need for me to go."

"Everyone needs some entertainment." Then she turned to her brother. "Do you need me to make snacks for you?"

"Aw, sis, you don't have to do that. But maybe some cookies would be good. Are you sure you have time?"

"Yes, of course. Come on, Ally. I'll need your help to get them made."

"Yay! I love making cookies!"

Lauren and Ally excused themselves and left Jack standing with Bill in the living room.

"So I'll see you at seven, Jack. Here's my address."

"Thanks, Bill. It was nice of you to think of me."

"We're glad to find you. It's no fun to play with just five people. Six is a much better number."

"Yeah, okay. Did—did Lauren say anything when you asked her about Ally?"

"No. But she won't mind. She likes little kids."

"Yeah." Jack waved goodbye to Bill and then debated what he should do. He could go to the kitchen for a chat, but Ally would be listening. That wouldn't be good. But this was the last invitation he could accept from the McNabbs. No matter what they offered.

"MAYBE NEXT TIME we can ask Daddy to come."

Lauren looked down at the child as they

entered the theater. She'd had the same thought herself, though for different reasons. The dim theater had made her remember their encounter in the dark kitchen on Friday night. She got gooseflesh just remembering how excited she felt being so near to him, touching him for mere seconds. What would she feel like sitting next to him for two hours?

But he wasn't her date tonight. Ally was. So she roped in her straying thoughts and led the little girl up several rows so she'd be able to see everything.

They shared a bag of popcorn and settled in for the movie.

When the previews of coming films started and the lights faded, Ally leaned against Lauren. "It's scary in the dark."

"No, it's not, baby. I'm right here beside you."

Ally giggled. "That's what Daddy calls me."

"I guess I learned it from him." She wrapped her arm around the child. "But you let me know if you get scared."

"Okay."

But Ally was fine. An hour and a half later, when the lights came on, Lauren looked down at her. "Did you enjoy it?"

"Yes, it was funny. I liked that little rabbit best."

"Me, too." They held hands as they exited the theater, and sang a song from the movie on the ride home. When they reached Lauren's apartment, she went in search of a shirt for Ally to sleep in.

"I know your daddy is going to take you home, but at least you can sleep until he gets here."

"But my PJs are at home."

"That's why I'm going to loan you something to sleep in. Come on, let's see what we can find."

A few minutes later, Ally was wearing one of Lauren's T-shirts. It came to her ankles and she held it up as if it were an evening gown. "I like your shirt," she told Lauren.

"I'm glad you do. It looks good on you."

The girl twirled like a princess at a ball.

Lauren giggled. "I'm going to make you a bed on the sofa. You can go to sleep while I watch television."

"You won't leave me?"

"No, sweetie, not until your daddy takes you home."

She got the child settled on the sofa on a sheet and pillow and covered her with a soft blanket. After she helped her say her prayers, she sat down beside her, turning on the television. In no time Ally fell asleep.

True to her word, Lauren stayed by her side, until a knock sounded on her door. Quietly she got up and went to the door. "I wasn't expecting you this early," she said as she opened it to Jack.

"I intended to be here by ten, but your brothers didn't want me to leave early."

She stepped aside so he could enter. "I can imagine. But Ally is doing fine. There was no need to hurry."

"I didn't want you to stay up late. Did she behave herself?"

"Absolutely. She was wonderful."

"I really appreciate your taking care of her, Lauren."

"It wasn't a problem."

"Yeah, but you should've gone out tonight, not me. I'm sure there's some man out there who would like an evening spent with you."

Lauren felt her cheeks turn red. "No. No one. I mean, I don't usually date much. My workload is heavy. That's one of the things the judge didn't like. He thought I wasn't taking enough time for—for other things."

"So he'd be very upset with the way you spent your evening."

"That doesn't matter."

Jack came toward her, invading her personal space. "The least I can do is give you a kiss."

"No! No, it isn't neces—"

But Jack didn't let her speak. He leaned forward and covered her lips with his. Gently, sweetly.

For a minute, everything around her faded and she tasted temptation. So tempted was she to give herself over to the kiss, to press herself against him and kiss him back. Instead, she drew back, her cheeks flaming, her pulse racing.

"Ally is asleep on the sofa," Lauren said hurriedly, looking away.

She could feel Jack's eyes on her as he stood there quietly. "Okay. I'll take her home now." He went to the sofa, scooped his child up, and strode toward the door. "Thanks again," he whispered just before he stepped out.

Lauren softly closed the door behind them. Then she leaned against it, thinking about the kiss Jack had given her. It had been amazing. But she wouldn't think about it again.

Definitely not again.

THE NEXT MORNING, Jack made sure he got up early enough to prepare breakfast for his little girl.

"Why are you cooking, Daddy?" Ally asked.

"So Lauren won't have to," he said, concentrating on the eggs he was scrambling in a pan.

"But she likes it," Ally pointed out.

"Yeah, but you're my little girl. I need to feed you breakfast."

"Okay, but Lolly won't like it."

"Too bad. Here are your eggs. Eat up."

"But, Daddy—"

"What, Ally?"

"Your eggs are hard. Lolly's are soft."

Jack held his patience. "Just eat the eggs, Ally. They're still good for you, even if I did cook them too long."

"Yes, Daddy."

When they reached Lauren's apartment,

Jack immediately announced, "Ally and I ate breakfast at home this morning. There's no need for you to cook."

"I didn't mind."

"Not necessary. Thanks anyway," he said as he walked back to the office to work. But he could hear his child, the traitor, mention that his eggs were too hard.

He hoped that didn't mean Lauren would cook more eggs for her. He'd have to make sure that didn't happen.

So a few minutes later, he went to the kitchen. "Mind if I get a drink of water?"

"No, not at all. I hesitate to mention it, but I also made a pot of coffee if you want some." Lauren had a cup of coffee in front of her as Ally colored in a coloring book across the table from her.

Jack mentally debated accepting a cup. In

the end, he couldn't turn it down. "Yeah, thanks, I'll take some."

She poured, steam rising from the liquid. His mouth watered. He hadn't taken the time to make coffee this morning. He seldom did, but he usually got a cup at whatever fast-food place he bought them breakfast.

He carried his coffee back to the study and put it on a shelf, after first taking a sip. Yeah, she made good coffee as well as soft eggs. What a woman!

And he wasn't even going to think about her looks. She was a beautiful woman, but even more important, she was very bright, an over-achiever if there ever was one. And in spite of her past, she was the last person to think of as a mommy. Like Ally's mother, she had other things on her agenda.

He squared his jaw and came to a decision.

He needed to find a school for his little girl. Further association with Lauren could only bring heartbreak.

He pulled out his cell phone and began making calls.

"I THINK THIS MORNING we should go visit that play school where Lila is going. Would you like to do that?" Lauren asked Ally.

"Okay. Can Daddy go?"

"Not this morning. But if you like it, we can tell him about it."

"Okay."

Just in case Jack came looking for Ally, Lauren left a note telling him they'd gone to run some errands. She figured that would satisfy him.

Then she and Ally got in her car and drove to the school. It wasn't even too far away from her apartment. Inside, they found everything bright and cheerful, a happy place. Ally saw Lila and waved as Lauren talked to the head of the school. She discovered they did have one opening, with the option of full day or half day.

Though she knew she had no right, she signed Ally up to come to school, initially on the half-day program, with the option of going all day in a couple of weeks. Then she collected the literature to take back to Jack. She only hoped he'd forgive her for doing so, but she wanted to help.

"What did you think, Ally?"

"I like it. They have good toys."

"Yes, that's important, and they start teaching you the alphabet, too. You'll need to know that when you start kindergarten. When is your birthday?"

"I forgot. Daddy said soon." Her face lit up as she remembered that remark.

"So you're almost four. That's very good. I hope Daddy is happy with us."

When they got back to the apartment, they found Jack pacing the floor. "Where have you been?" he demanded.

"Didn't you find the note?" Lauren asked.

"Yes, I found the note! You think that explains everything? You've gone to run some errands? That tells me nothing! I've got an appointment for Ally in half an hour!"

"An appointment for what?"

"To go visit a school. I'm putting her back in an organized program. She needs to get ready for kindergarten."

"I agree—" Lauren began, but he cut her off.

"What you think doesn't matter. You're not

her mother and never will be. You have a career that comes first. My child needs—"

"We went to visit a school that I heard about at the grocery store. I didn't want to tell you until I was sure it was a good school where Ally would be happy."

"You did what? You took her to visit a school without telling me? I'm her father! How dare you do that! You had no right to take charge of her life—or mine, either, for that matter!"

"I was just trying to help."

"No one asked for your help. You're the one who wanted to take care of Ally."

"And I still do, but I'm looking at the future. I won't be available in another couple of weeks and I didn't want you to be stranded with no place to take her."

"That's my job!" Jack roared.

They both fell silent when they realized Ally

was crying. Jack squatted down in front of his daughter. "Ally, honey, what's wrong?"

"You're fighting. I don't want you to fight!" Then she buried her face in her father's shoulder.

Jack stood, lifting Ally with him. "I'm not working the rest of today," he muttered, with a challenge in his voice.

"All right, but I need to—"

"No. I need to see about my child." With Ally in his arms, he walked out the door.

Lauren remembered the car seat was still in her car. Grabbing her keys, she followed him out. "Jack, I have her car seat. Just a minute and I'll transfer it to your truck."

She unlocked her car, retrieved Ally's car seat and carried it to the backseat of Jack's truck. After she secured it, she stepped back so he could put Ally in it.

"Goodbye, sweetheart. I'll see you tomorrow," she said to Ally.

Ally looked at her with tearful eyes, not responding to her smile.

"Don't cry, angel. Everything will be all right." Lauren kept a smile on her lips even though she wanted to cry, too. She didn't like it when they fought, either.

"Oh, Jack, here are the brochures from the place I visited. They only had one spot open. I know I shouldn't have, but I signed Ally up for that spot. If you like the other place, call and let them know."

He glared at her, but he took the brochures with him as he circled the truck and got in.

She wished he'd forgive her at once. But he appeared to still be very angry. She'd only done what any sensible woman would have done. At least, any sensible mother.

But that was the problem. She wasn't Ally's mother. Which made Lauren stop and think. What did she know about Ally's mother? Jack had never mentioned the woman. They must've had a bitter divorce. And how did he end up with Ally?

Lauren knew the court system. Mothers usually got custody of small children. And a newborn would certainly have been awarded to the mother if she'd fought for her child. What woman wouldn't? Unless she was a druggie or lower than that.

Lauren went to her computer and started searching for documents that would tell the story of Allison Mason. Three hours later, she found what she was looking for. Ally's mother had willingly given her daughter to Jack, her father. Unless Jack paid her for his child, there was no explanation given for her behavior.

Lauren turned off her computer and came back to the kitchen. It was two o'clock and she had forgotten to eat lunch. In such a short time, she'd gotten used to sharing lunch with Jack and his daughter. Now she had to eat alone.

Somehow, lunch didn't seem as appealing alone. Was Jack going to come back and finish the job? Would he bring Ally back?

She desperately wanted answers to those questions, but she had no way of knowing.

Except to wait for tomorrow.

Chapter Six

Jack didn't look at the brochure Lauren had handed him until he parked his truck at the school he'd found. Then he discovered they had found the same school.

He got Ally out of her seat and carried her to the door. "Did you like this school when you came earlier?"

"Yes, it's nice. And Lila goes to school here."

"Who is Lila?"

"She's from my old school."

"Okay." He opened the door and entered to find a receptionist on duty. "Good morning. I have an appointment at—"

Before he could finish, the receptionist said, "Oh, sir, I'm sorry, but the director promised that spot to someone else."

Jack tried to explain. "Yes, I think she promised it to—"

"That girl. That's who we promised it to," said another woman's voice behind them.

Ally waved to the woman.

"Hello, you must be Ally's father. We're so glad to meet you," the older lady said as she drew closer. "I'm Mrs. Applebaum, the director. I talked to Ally this morning with your wife. She's delightful."

His wife? Jack wanted to explain that Lauren McNabb was not his wife—nor would she ever be—but how could he? It would make him look like a terrible father. Or a neglectful one. Instead, he went along with it. "Uh, thanks, yes, she said she really liked the school, but I wanted to see it myself."

"Certainly. We approve of both parents visiting the school."

The director took him on a little tour and he agreed with Lauren. It was bright and clean, and the children appeared happy.

"Can she start tomorrow?"

"Well, yes, actually. We can take Ally tomorrow morning. And who will pick her up? You or her mother?"

"Actually, it's—it's her stepmother, and I'll be picking her up. I need her to stay all day."

"All right. Your wife told us she would pick her up for the next two weeks."

"Her plans changed unexpectedly."

"Of course, that happens. But you'll both be able to attend our fall get-together, won't you? We're having it tomorrow night, so it's a perfect time for the two of you to meet other parents."

"Yes, of course." Jack figured he'd explain that his "wife" didn't feel well and couldn't make it.

"Very good. I'll call her about what she should bring. It's a potluck dinner. Everyone is assigned to bring something. I have her number here. Lauren, isn't it?"

"Yeah, that's her." He felt like a sinking ship, taking on water faster than he could bail.

The woman extended her hand for a shake. "All right, then. We'll see Ally in the morning and both of you tomorrow night."

"Yes, thanks." Jack hurried Ally out before she could tell them Lauren wasn't her stepmother.

Once he was behind the wheel, he headed back to Lauren's apartment. He had to prepare her for Mrs. Applebaum's call and her needed appearance tomorrow night.

"Daddy, did that lady say Lolly was my mommy?"

"Yeah. She got confused."

"But didn't you say the same thing?"

"Baby, I had to agree with her or they might not've let you in the school, and it seems like a nice school."

"Okay."

He looked in the rearview mirror at his little girl, a smile on her face. "That doesn't mean she is your mommy—because she's not."

"I know, Daddy. It's all right."

How ridiculous for his child to be reassuring him, Jack thought. But he needed the reassurance, that she understood what was happening.

When they reached the apartment, Jack got Ally out of her chair and carried her to Lauren's door and knocked.

When Lauren opened the door, he started explaining. "The director of the school is going to call. She thinks we're married and—"

The phone interrupted him.

With a strange look at him, Lauren moved to the phone. "Hello?"

After a moment, she said, "Well, actually, I use my maiden name professionally. Lauren McNabb. Yes, of course. Tomorrow night? Certainly. Oh, we don't bring our children? No, that won't be a problem. What shall I bring?"

After a moment, she said, "I can bring chicken spaghetti and a carrot cake. No, it's not a problem. Yes, thank you. We'll be there at six-thirty."

Lauren turned around and stared at Jack, noting that he'd turned on the television for Ally in the living room.

"I know. I shouldn't have, but it got all confusing. I didn't want to tell them you were messing in my business. I thought it would be easier to just let them think we were married. But I didn't know about the get-together. But by the time I did, I was already committed."

"So I'm Ally's mother?"

"Her stepmother. That seemed more likely. I really appreciate you going along with me on this. Once we do the get-together, we'll be through. You won't have to do anything else."

"Right," Lauren drawled.

"No, I told them your plans had changed and Ally would go all day to the school."

"What about tomorrow night? Do you have a babysitter?"

Jack's eyes widened. He hadn't considered that. "I don't have anyone to babysit. I guess I can call one of those services, but I hate to use them."

"Why don't I call James and see if he and Cheryl can sit for you?"

"Do you think they would?"

"I think so. They both thought Ally was very cute. You can bring her here and let them watch her. We shouldn't be too late."

"I'd rather have them come to my place so she can go to bed on time."

"All right. I'll call James at work. Just a minute."

Jack waited anxiously while Lauren talked to James. When she hung up the phone, she turned and said, "He agreed. He's calling Cheryl now. But he said he'd be there with Cheryl unless something happened."

"What could happen?" Jack demanded.

"Nothing, Jack. They'll be there. You'll need to call him tonight and give him your address and the time you need them there."

"All right. Thanks, Lauren. I hadn't thought about a sitter."

"It's hard to think of everything when you're getting used to a new wife," she said with a wicked smile.

A rueful smile played about his lips. "I know I'm going to pay for my lies. But I thought it would be an easy way out."

"Maybe. We'll see how it goes tomorrow night."

"I'm sorry you have to fix so much. I'll pay the grocery bill."

"I already have a pan of chicken spaghetti in the freezer, so I'll just have to make another cake."

"Too bad you can't take what's left of the first cake."

Lauren laughed. "They'd boo me out of the

room. But you and Ally can help out by eating another piece after lunch."

"All right, if you'll let me buy lunch. We can go to the Chili's down the street. Deal?"

Lauren seemed to be considering his offer. Then she grinned and said, "Deal."

"THIS IS NOT a date," she muttered to herself as she stared at her image in the mirror. She'd prepared for the evening as if it were a date, but she knew it wasn't. She had brought this situation on herself. Jack had apologized, but she knew if she hadn't taken Ally to the school and asked them to hold the spot for her, she wouldn't be going tonight to play the role of her stepmother.

"Lauren Mason. Hmm, I wonder if Perry Mason would mind if I played the role of a lawyer named after him?" she said and then laughed. She was being silly.

With another touch of lipstick, she turned away from the mirror. It was time to gather her contributions to the evening. Jack would be here in a minute.

Their lunch the day before had taken a long time. They'd talked about their childhoods— her with her brothers and sisters, him an only child. His parents had moved to Florida five years ago. They'd come to see Ally when she was a baby, but Jack hadn't been as welcoming as he should have been. He'd thought they disapproved of Ally.

Lauren decided she preferred her big family to his lonely life. Her parents might not be alive, but she had her brothers and sisters.

The doorbell rang and she drew a deep breath before she headed to the front door. Swinging it open, she smiled at Jack. "You're right on time."

"Good. I've been sitting outside waiting. I didn't want to get here early."

"You didn't have to do that. Come on in. I've got to get the food ready."

Jack followed her into the kitchen.

"The cake is in the carrier. I'll get the chicken spaghetti out of the oven." Using mitts, she took the casserole out and set it on the cabinet. Then she covered it with foil. "Okay, I'm ready."

Jack told her again how much he appreciated her work.

"Please, Jack, it's no big deal."

"I think it is. Anyway, be sure you don't forget your role. We don't want to spoil everything now."

"No, we don't. Did Ally enjoy school today?"

"Yes. But she missed you."

"I told her we could spend some time together Saturday, while you run your errands."

"I'll think about it."

"Jack, I understand why you were so cautious about Ally and me, but I've explained that I'm not her mommy, just a friend."

"Yeah, if she believes you."

"I can't just walk away from her."

"You will when you go back to work and get involved in your work. I've seen it happen before."

"Is that what happened to her mother?"

"No."

Clearly he didn't want to talk about it, so Lauren dropped the subject. They were quiet until they were at his truck.

"Well, here we go, madam wife."

At his words Lauren swallowed a sudden lump in her throat. "I think we should be careful and not say too much."

"You're probably right."

They rode quietly the five minutes it took to reach the school.

"Looks like they've had a good turnout," Jack muttered.

"Yes. Everyone has learned the importance of being involved in his child's education."

"So, did you go to the parent meetings when your brothers and sisters had one?"

"Yes, of course."

"You must've felt out of place."

"It didn't matter. I was intent on being there for them and everyone got used to me showing up."

Jack drew a deep breath. "I wish I was as experienced at these things."

"You'll do fine, Jack. Remember, it's for Ally."

"Yeah."

They entered the school room, cleared now

of the toys Ally had liked. Across the back of the room was a long table to hold all the food. Tables and chairs filled the rest of the room so they could all sit and eat.

On the way to the back, Jack and Lauren met the director, who greeted them warmly. Then she introduced them to several parents standing nearby who were wearing name tags.

"As soon as you put down the food, we need to get name tags for you, too. It helps everyone get to know one another."

They noticed their name tags each bore a picture of Ally.

"When did they get a picture of her?" Jack wondered.

"I'm sure they used a digital camera and printed it on the computer," Lauren whispered. "But it's cute, isn't it?"

"Yeah." He pinned the tag on his shirt. "Want me to pin yours on?"

"No, I've got it."

"That's probably best," Jack muttered, but he watched her as she put the tag on her chest.

"Hello, I'm Gregory Black, Jason's father," a man said as he stuck out his hand to Lauren. She shook his hand and introduced her husband, not flinching when she used that word.

They moved through the room, meeting the parents, until they were all told to fall into line for the potluck buffet.

The evening was interesting, Lauren thought. When it was time for dessert, she got up and began cutting her cake. Knowing Jack would want some, she put aside a piece for him. When he reached the table and realized all the cake was gone, he was upset.

"I saved you a piece," she said, offering him a saucer with the last piece of carrot cake.

The lady next to Jack laughed. "That kind of loyalty deserves a kiss, young man."

Jack grinned at her. "You're right, it does." He flashed a look at Lauren and leaned forward.

Lauren knew she had to play along. What would a little kiss mean, anyway? She leaned forward to meet him, her lips puckered. When their lips met, she realized even a simple kiss with Jack meant something. Then, suddenly, she felt his hand around the back of her neck, pulling her into the kiss.

The kiss deepened and without thinking, Lauren put her arms around Jack's neck. Her mouth opened to meet his and she was lost in his kiss.

"Woo-hoo, look at these two! They must be

newly married," a woman nearby called out, and Lauren jumped back, as did Jack.

"Uh, yeah, sorry," Jack muttered and took his piece of cake to the table to eat.

Lauren didn't know where to look.

"Don't worry," the woman said. "You just made us all jealous, that's all. It's been a while since my husband even thought to give me a peck, much less a kiss like that."

Lauren gave her an awkward smile. "I'm sure Jack will get that way, too, after a while."

"They all do, honey."

Lauren smiled at the woman, who didn't look a lot older than Lauren.

Her eyes encountered Jack as she scanned the room. She immediately looked away. He didn't. She pretended an intense interest in what was left as a dessert choice. In the end, she gave up on a dessert. She didn't need one anyway.

Taking her serving container to the sink, she rinsed it. As she turned around, the director, Mrs. Applebaum, stepped to her side.

"I just wanted to welcome you and Jack again. You're a lovely couple, obviously well-suited. Ally is a lucky little girl."

"Thank you, Mrs. Applebaum. I think Ally will be very happy here."

"What kind of work do you do?"

"I'm an attorney."

"Oh, really? How interesting that you're married to a carpenter."

"Jack is more than a carpenter. He's an artist. His work is outstanding."

"Oh, yes, of course. I was thinking about asking him to make some storage cabinets here. Do you think he'll be interested?"

"I'm not sure. He has a list of customers waiting for him to get to them." She smiled at the woman and moved away.

"What did she say to make you angry?" Jack asked as he stepped to Lauren's side.

She jumped, surprised by his closeness.

"Are you okay?"

"Yes, of course."

"So are you going to tell me what she said?"

She lifted her chin and shook her head. "I don't think so."

"So it wasn't about our marriage?"

"Not at all."

"She must've said something mean about lawyers," Jack guessed, watching her closely.

"Yes, that's it. She doesn't like lawyers."

Jack frowned. "Maybe I'd better go have a word with her."

"No!" Lauren said, grabbing his arm. "No, don't do that. People always think badly of lawyers. Just let it go."

"I don't think you should have to put up

with insults about your job. We could pull Ally out of the school."

"No. It's a great school and we're lucky to get Ally in. It won't be a problem."

"You're sure?" Jack asked, staring at her.

"I'm sure. Are you ready to go?"

"Yeah, but we have to say goodbye and get your dish."

"Yes, I'll—I need you to come help me." She didn't want him to have a chance to speak to Mrs. Applebaum without her. She led the way to the back table, where the dishes were waiting to be picked up. "Can you carry the casserole dish?"

"Sure."

He picked up the long casserole dish as she picked up the cake plate. Together they walked to the exit where Mrs. Applebaum was waiting to say goodbye.

"Thank you for a lovely evening," Lauren said.

"I'm delighted you could come. You both were a welcome addition to our little family." Mrs. Applebaum gave them both a big smile.

"Yes, thank you," Jack said.

Lauren breathed a big sigh of relief when they reached Jack's truck. Jack had helped her in and closed the door to go to the other side, so he couldn't hear her. He was doing work he loved, just as she was, and she wouldn't let anyone think any less of him.

Once they were both in the truck, Lauren thought the interior of the vehicle seemed to shrink. All she could think about was the kiss they'd shared in front of all those people. It had certainly taken her by surprise.

She looked at Jack out of the corner of her eye. There was no question he was good-looking.

She'd noticed that the first moment she'd met him, but then she'd been distracted by Ally.

"Are you tired?" Jack asked.

"What? Oh, no, I didn't work today."

"Yeah, I know. But you're being very quiet."

"I guess I got talked out at the meeting."

"Yeah. There were a lot of big talkers there tonight. I was told by four different men that they were vital to their company's success."

"Oh, really?"

"Yeah. Then they wanted to know what I did for a living."

"Did you tell them?"

"I told them I was a carpenter."

Lauren drew in a deep breath. "But you're much more than that, Jack, and you know it."

"I don't need to advertise my work at my daughter's school."

"I know, but—"

"It's no big deal, Lauren."

"No, I guess not," she said as he pulled into her place on Yellow Rose Lane. "There's no need to get out, Jack," she hurriedly added as she reached for her door.

"I've got to help you carry the dishes, at least."

"Oh, I forgot."

When they reached her apartment, she hurried to the kitchen to put the cake plate down and turned to take the casserole dish from Jack.

He gave it to her, but when she turned around to tell him good-night, he wrapped his arms around her and his mouth covered hers.

Chapter Seven

Jack wasn't sure he'd have a job when he got to Lauren's apartment the next morning. But he pretended all was normal.

Which was far from the truth. His insides were jumping as he thought about the kiss they'd shared last night. True, he'd initiated the kiss, but she hadn't resisted. In fact, her arms had been around his neck when he lifted his mouth from hers.

He'd wanted to kiss her again, but he feared he'd scoop her up and head for the nearest bed if he had. He didn't think that would be appropriate.

After dropping Ally off at school, he drove slowly to Lauren's apartment and sat in his truck for several minutes. Then, calling himself all kinds of a coward, he opened his truck door and walked toward her apartment. Banging on the door, he stood there waiting for his sentence.

"Oh, good, you're here," Lauren said as she opened the door.

Jack noticed at once that she was dressed in a narrow black skirt, white tailored blouse and a red jacket. She was wearing stockings and heels, and her hair was pinned up. Not at all the casual Lauren he'd seen for the past two weeks.

"Sorry, but I have to go downtown today. Can you lock up when you leave? Just push the lock in the door. Your lunch is in the refrigerator, a roast beef sandwich. If you need more, find whatever you want. Thanks," she said over her shoulder as she slipped past him, leaving him no opportunity to say anything.

Jack stood there in the open door, watching her almost run to her car, not bothering to look back. She obviously had other things on her mind than their kiss. Unlike him. She was going back to the office long before she was supposed to. Judge Robinson must've changed his mind.

Jack went back to the study, prepared to go to work. But the image of Lauren remained fresh in his mind. Though she was as beautiful this morning as she'd been that first morning, she was more distant now. He preferred her in casual clothes, relaxed, smiling.

But maybe it was a good idea to appear distant out in the world. He didn't want some other man hitting on her, some other lawyer trying to make time with her.

Wait a minute! What was he thinking? It

wasn't as if he was planning on having a relationship with her! Of course not. He'd just kissed her. That was all.

Damn it! He'd kiss her again if he had half a chance. Her lips were addictive. But obviously, he wasn't going to have the chance today, so he might as well get on with the job.

LAUREN CALLED HERSELF all kinds of a coward for running away from Jack. His kiss had knocked her for a loop. After he'd walked out, she'd had to fight herself not to run after him. You would think she hadn't been kissed before. She had, and expertly, at that.

But Jack's kiss had reached deep down inside her and frightened her...and made her want more.

So she'd pretended to be too busy to stay home today. Besides, she had nothing to do at home. Everything was clean, organized and up-to-date. So she thought up something to research in the legal library at her office. Then she'd see if anyone was free for lunch. After that, she'd go shopping. Buying new clothes would make her feel good.

Of course, the first person she ran into at the office was Judge Robinson.

"What are you doing here, young lady?" the older man demanded.

"I just wanted to look up something in the law library, sir. I didn't think you'd mind if I didn't stay too long."

"I wanted you to have complete rest."

"I have had. But I've run out of things to do."

"You could develop a hobby."

"I've been doing the crossword puzzle each morning," she volunteered, offering a smile.

"Humph! How's Jack working out?"

Lauren fought to keep the blush from her cheeks. "His work is wonderful. And he's right on schedule."

"So you'll have a nice home office?"

"Yes, a terrific one. I can't wait to move in."

"Good. He's a fine craftsman...and a nice man."

"Yes, he certainly is. And Ally is a delight."

"Who is Ally? Has the boy gotten married?"

"No, Ally is his little girl. She's almost four years old."

"You met his daughter?"

"Yes, he brought her that first morning." She almost continued the saga until she realized it might draw too much attention. "Her day care had shut down, so he brought her with him that first morning."

"Oh. That must've been awkward. That's not like Jack."

"No, it was fine."

"Well, I'm glad things are working out for you. And you're getting plenty of rest?"

"Absolutely." Not counting last night.

"Because you look a little tired this morning." He stared at her.

"I watched a late movie last night. Then I woke up early this morning. I'll take a nap this afternoon. I only plan on being here a couple of hours."

"Good. Okay, then, I'll see you in a couple of weeks."

"Yes, thank you, Judge." She slipped into the law library as soon as she could. She didn't want to visit with anyone else until she'd regained her composure.

She went to lunch with a couple of the other lawyers. Then she went shopping. In the past, her shopping trips had been to refurbish her work wardrobe as a necessity. Today, she found herself looking more at leisure clothes, thinking about Jack's reaction to them.

"You're being silly," she told herself. Jack wouldn't be around that much longer.

That thought depressed her and she left the mall and drove home. It was almost five o'clock. Jack was probably already gone. But her heart lifted when she saw his truck still parked in front of her apartment.

Unlocking the front door, she walked straight back to her study to discover Jack working.

"Isn't it kind of late for you to still be working?" she asked.

He spun around, almost dropping the level in his hand. "I didn't hear you come in."

"It's almost five o'clock. What time do you pick up Ally?"

"Damn! I should've been there by four-thirty! I've got to hurry. By the time I get packed up—"

"Want me to go get her? Both our names are on the card, so they'll let her come with me."

"Do you mind? It would take me fifteen minutes just to get all my tools in the truck."

"I'll be right back with her," Lauren said cheerfully and dashed out of her apartment. In five minutes she was at the day care and had Ally giving her a big hug.

"I missed you," she whispered to the little girl.

"Me, too."

"She was getting worried," Mrs. Applebaum said.

"Her dad had to work a little late today, so I got here as soon as I could."

"Well, we're open until six, so it's not a problem."

"Thank you. Goodbye."

Once they were in Lauren's car, she told Ally that her dad had forgotten the time. "You know how involved he gets when he's on a job."

"I know," Ally said, nodding. "What did you fix him for lunch?"

"I made him a roast beef sandwich. What did you have for lunch?"

"They served us hot dogs and green beans. And we had ice cream for dessert."

"That sounds good."

"It was okay, but I like your lunches better."

Lauren smiled at Ally, wishing she could feed her lunch again.

When they got back to the apartment, Jack was all packed up. "Thanks, Lauren. How about we take you out to dinner to say thank you?"

"Oh, no, that's not necessary." She avoided his gaze.

"Oh, please, Lolly? I haven't seen you all day long! Dinner would be fun."

Lauren couldn't resist Ally's eager look. "Well, I could go, I suppose, but you don't have to buy my dinner, Jack. I can pay for my own."

"No, you picked up Ally for me, so I think it's only fair that I treat you."

They all got in the truck and drove to a nearby casual restaurant. Once they were seated, Ally asked, "Why are you wearing dress-up clothes?"

"I went downtown this morning. I had some work to do."

"Yeah, she was gone all day, honey. I was by myself." Jack sent a look at Lauren that she hurriedly avoided.

"But you got more work done, didn't you, Daddy?"

"Yeah, I did."

"He always tells me he gets more work done when he's alone. But I always think it's more fun if someone else is there."

"So you need to look for a job that includes other people," Lauren said with a smile. "I feel the same way."

"So I can become a… What do you do?" Ally asked.

"I'm an attorney, sweetheart."

"So I can be an attorney, too!" Ally said.

"Absolutely, if you want to go to school a long time."

Ally looked at her. "How long?"

"Nineteen years," Lauren said with a laugh. "It takes a lot of work."

"And a lot of money," Jack added.

"How long did you go to school, Daddy?"

"Just sixteen years," he said.

"They're both a long time," Ally said. "That's more than I am old."

"I'm afraid so, Ally, but it will go by like a flash," Lauren told her.

"But I haven't even started kindergarten yet!"

Both adults laughed, meeting glances over their dinner plates.

After dinner, they were leaving the restaurant when they ran into Mrs. Applebaum coming in. They exchanged greetings and moved on. Once they were in the truck, Jack said, "Remind me to avoid that restaurant from now on."

"Yes, we probably need a list of local places where she likes to go. Otherwise, you'll never be able to take a date out for a meal."

"Unless you're my date," he murmured.

Lauren turned to argue with him, and he dropped a kiss on her lips.

"Just a thought," he whispered.

She turned away. She didn't want him to see the happiness that thought brought her.

Ally, sitting in the backseat, said nothing. Lauren didn't want to turn around and face the child. Maybe, if they were lucky, Ally hadn't noticed the kiss.

When they reached her apartment, she opened the truck door, saying at once, "There's no need to get out. I'll see you tomorrow."

And she ran inside.

"DADDY, WHY DID you kiss Lolly?"

Jack looked in the rearview mirror at his little girl. "Um, because I like her."

"Does she like you?"

"I don't know for sure, but I hope so."

"Does that mean she'll be my mommy?" Ally asked eagerly.

"No! No, it doesn't mean that. Sometimes daddies just like to kiss someone."

"I like Lolly a lot."

"So you give her a kiss, too, right?"

"Yes, but not on the mouth. You told me to kiss you on the cheek, not the mouth."

"That's right. Only adults kiss people on the mouth if they really like them."

"Oh."

"How was school today?" he asked in an effort to steer the conversation into safer waters.

"It was okay. But I liked going out to dinner with Lolly."

"Yeah, me, too."

"Can we do it again tomorrow night?"

"No, tomorrow is Saturday. I don't work tomorrow."

"Lolly said we would have a play date on Saturday. Did she mean this Saturday?"

No, he remarked to himself, they were too busy doing other things.

Like kissing.

LAUREN THOUGHT about her promise to Ally. Today was Saturday. Would it be too forward of her to call and ask for Ally today?

She decided to call anyway. She found the number she'd been given for Jack and dialed.

"Hello?"

"Ally, is that you? It's Lolly."

"Lolly! I wanted to call you, but Daddy said you'd still be asleep."

"No, I'm awake. I wondered if you wanted to go shopping with me and have lunch while your daddy runs errands?"

"Yes!" Ally responded.

"Honey, you have to ask your daddy."

"Oh. Just a minute."

Jack, who was in the shower, first learned of the call when the bathroom door opened and Ally called out, "Daddy?"

He stuck his head around the shower curtain. "What is it, Ally?"

"It's Lolly on the phone. She wants—"

"I'll be right there."

He hurriedly dried himself and wrapped his robe around him. Then he went to the phone. "Hello?"

"Jack, I wondered if Ally could come shopping with me while you ran errands. I'll bring her back after lunch."

"That's very nice of you, but I don't have many errands to run. How about I meet you two for lunch?"

"I—I suppose we could do that."

"Great. When will you pick her up?"

"Is ten o'clock okay?"

"It's perfect, and you can let me know then where to meet you for lunch."

"All right. Tell Ally I'll see her at ten."

"Will do."

He hung up the phone and did just that. "Lauren is coming at ten o'clock. I hope you have something nice to wear."

"I'll go see," Ally assured him and raced down the hall.

He ran after her to his room. He had some sprucing up to do, too.

At nine fifty, Ally was in a play dress, her shoes and socks in place and her hair brushed. Jack was freshly shaved and wearing a nice shirt and slacks, ready to meet Lauren. They both paced the floor though they were several minutes early.

"Shouldn't she be here by now?" Ally asked.

"In a few minutes," Jack said. "We just have

to be patient." He drew a deep breath, prepared to demonstrate to his daughter just how patient he could be. Then he saw Lauren's car pull into their driveway.

"Here she is," he said, and then grabbed his daughter's arm as she turned to run outside. "When someone comes to pick you up, we let them come to the door. Lauren's never seen your house. You could offer to show her your room."

He'd made sure Ally's room was neat and presentable just for that purpose. He was proud of his house. He'd bought it after he'd taken charge of Ally.

Ally ran to the door when the doorbell rang.

"Hi, Lolly. Would you like to see my room?"

"I'd love to see your room, Ally," Lauren said with a big smile. It shrank a little when she encountered Jack, but at least it remained in place.

Ally led Lauren down the hall, followed by Jack, to show her her bedroom. "See? I have my baby dolls over here, and all my clothes are hung up. Daddy said we had to do that."

"Yes, and it all looks lovely, sweetie. I guess you play with your toys over here. It's a very nice room."

"Thank you. Now can we go?"

"I tried to teach her manners," Jack muttered.

"And she did very well, Jack," Lauren said with a smile.

He liked that smile. Returning it, he took a step closer, but she grabbed Ally's hand and moved past him. "We're off to shop now. Is there anything Ally needs?"

"If you find some clothes that will be good for winter at school, that would be good. Here, take my credit card."

"No. I'll use mine and you can pay me back."

"All right. Where do I meet you for lunch?"

"How about the food court? We'll find a table near the clock and see you there around twelve."

"Okay. Behave, Ally."

"I will, Daddy!"

Jack watched them go, a little jealous that he wasn't included in the shopping trip. He and Ally had made shopping trips before, but he didn't think they had as much fun as she and Lauren would have. But a couple of hours and he'd see Lauren again. He could hardly wait.

THE FOOD COURT was already beginning to fill up. He managed to snag a table for four near the clock and sat down to watch for his two favorite girls.

"Well, hello there. Are you eating alone today?" a purring voice asked, drawing his attention.

Jack looked up to see a beautiful young woman wearing way too much makeup standing by his table.

"Actually, I'm waiting for someone," he said with a dismissive smile.

She didn't take the hint. "I could keep you company until they come."

"No, thanks. I need to look for them."

"What do they look like?"

He was getting irritated with the persistent woman. "A beautiful woman and a very cute little girl. I'll recognize them when I see them."

"Oh, too bad. If you want my number, I can give it to you."

"No, thank you."

"Too bad. Your loss."

With a seductive smile, she moved away.

"Daddy, who is that lady?"

Jack spun around to find Lauren and Ally

standing a few feet from the table. "I don't know."

"Then why were you talking to her?" Ally asked. "You said I shouldn't talk to strangers."

"Yes, Jack," Lauren added, "we don't want to intrude if you have something else to do." She emphasized the "something else."

He stood and put his arms around Lauren. "I have nothing else to do, but you'd better give me a kiss to convince *her.*" Then he pulled her into his arms.

Chapter Eight

To his surprise and gratification, Lauren kissed him back.

Smiling, he teased, "Not bad for someone who's angry."

"I'm not angry, but—"

He halted her remark and turned to his daughter. "What did you buy?" he asked Ally as he pulled out a chair for Lauren.

"We bought me two things for winter. They're beautiful!" she announced as he helped her into a chair.

"Good for you," he told Lauren. "She never likes what I buy her."

"She told me."

"Traitor!" Jack teased.

"You always say they'll look better once we get them home, but they don't." Ally opened the sack and wanted to take everything out.

"Not now, sweetie," Lauren said. "Let's wait until we get back to the apartment."

"Oh, you mean because of the panties?" Ally whispered.

"Right," Lauren agreed, her cheeks red.

"I should've known. She loves underwear," Jack whispered, too.

"You could've warned me. I didn't know."

"Yeah, I should've, but I forgot all about it when you called. All I could think about was seeing you again."

"Jack!" Lauren admonished, this time unable to keep the blush from her cheeks.

His gaze remained fixed on her face, loving

the way she looked. "No one tried to pick you up, did they?"

Ally frowned. "Why would someone do that? We didn't fall."

"That's the expression when some guy comes along and wants your phone number." He kept his gaze fixed on Lauren.

"Lolly! You gave your phone number to one man!" Ally accused.

"You did?" Jack asked.

"In that store they ask for your phone number when they put the sale in the computer," Lauren hurriedly said. "The man was seventy if he was a day!"

"Oh. Then I guess that's all right," Jack agreed with a big grin.

"Jack Mason, you're being difficult! You were the one flirting, not me!"

"The only one I've been flirting with is you, honey. Only you."

"Daddy likes you, Lolly. He told me." Ally watched the two of them like a bird looking for a particularly large worm.

"Ally, don't interfere in what's going on here," Jack said, still staring at Lauren.

"Yes. It's a game men play that doesn't mean anything," Lauren responded.

Ally had already been patient. Now she changed her mind. "I'm hungry. Are we going to eat?"

"Right away. What would you like, baby?" Jack asked.

"Daddy, I'm over here," Ally complained.

Too late he realized he was still gazing into Lauren's chocolate eyes.

AFTER LUNCH they headed to Lauren's apartment. Ally promised to try on her new outfits to show her daddy how beautiful they were.

She immediately dragged Lauren into her bedroom so she could change in private.

Jack complained about being shut out, but he settled on the sofa to await Ally's modeling show. He raved about the first outfit. It was warm and stylish, he said.

Lauren wondered if he really knew it was stylish, or just used the word to please his daughter. She and Ally went back to change into the second outfit.

The phone rang and Lauren picked up the extension in the bedroom.

"Lauren, please help me. They say I killed him but I didn't!"

"Who is this?" Lauren asked in confusion.

"It's Robin! George is dead!"

"Okay, take a deep breath," she told Robin Amos, a friend of her sister Reggie's. "Where are you?"

"I'm at the p-police station. They think I killed my husband!"

"Listen to me, Robin. If they ask you any more questions, tell them you're waiting for your attorney to arrive." She checked her watch. "I'll be there in twenty minutes."

She hung up the phone and took off the polo shirt she was wearing. Ally stared at her, but she didn't even think to explain her actions. She put on a white tailored shirt and tucked it into her black pants. Then she pulled on a red jacket and stepped into other shoes. Then she grabbed her briefcase and headed for the door.

"Where are you going, Lolly?"

Lauren looked at the child in confusion. "Oh, Ally, I'm sorry, but I have to go. I'll tell your father."

When she reached the living room, she

started talking at once. "Jack, I have an emergency. Please lock the door when you leave."

By that time, she'd reached the front door and was through it, pulling the door to behind her in spite of Jack's questions. Then she ran to her car and headed to rescue Robin.

JACK STARED at the front door, the questions stopping when it was obvious he wasn't going to get answers. Ally came back to the living room, wearing the second outfit.

"Do you know where Lauren went?" he asked her.

"No. She told someone named Robin not to talk to the police until she got there. Is that true, Daddy?"

"Is what true, honey?"

"I thought I was supposed to be friendly with the police and do what they say."

"Yes, you are, but if they think you did something bad, it might be best to talk to your attorney first."

Jack sat there thinking about what Ally had told him. Obviously it was an emergency situation, but he was irritated that Lauren ditched them without an explanation.

"Good thing you're here, isn't it, Daddy? Otherwise I'd be here all alone."

"Yeah, and I don't like that. Lauren should've been more responsible."

"But, Daddy, she knew you would take care of me. It's just like yesterday when you worked too late and let Lolly come pick me up. She filled in for you. Today, you fill in for her."

"I guess, but she could've explained."

"I think she was in a hurry."

"Yeah." He checked his irritation in front of his daughter, then changed the subject.

"That's a great outfit, baby. You and Lauren did some good shopping. Go change back into your clothes so we can go home."

"Okay."

Ally did as she was told and Jack sat on the sofa, steaming because Lauren put her work before him and his daughter. Their lovely day had been ruined.

He realized whoever had called had an emergency, but Lauren shouldn't be on call like a medical doctor. She was an attorney! He hadn't expected her to work for another two weeks. And he'd conveniently forgotten that when she went back to work, things would change.

"I'm ready, Daddy. I didn't leave anything in the bedroom, either. I didn't want Lolly to think I'm messy."

"That's nice, baby. Let's go."

"Daddy, are you mad at Lolly?"

"I just think she should've shown more consideration for you. After all, she asked you to go shopping with her."

"But, Daddy, she didn't know that person would call. If one of your friends called with an emergency, you'd leave me somewhere safe and go at once."

"How do you know, baby?" He scooped her up in his arms, taking the large sack that held her purchases. "That hasn't happened since you were born."

"I just know, Daddy. You rescued that puppy one time and found its home. You wouldn't let anyone suffer."

"I hope not. Let's go home. I'm tired."

"Me, too. I miss Lolly already."

"Yeah, but it looks like she's going to be busy from now on."

"How do you know?" Ally asked as they went through the door.

"Because she's gone back to work, and she never takes time off from work."

ROBIN AMOS was a sad figure when Lauren reached her in the police station. She was sitting in a room all alone, slumped in a chair.

"Robin?" Lauren said at once. "Are you all right?"

"I guess, but…George is dead."

"I know. I'm sorry about George. Can you tell me what happened?"

Robin sobbed, and Lauren reached out and took her hand. "Things are going to be all right. It will just take a little time."

"I'm not sure things will ever be the same."

Lauren looked Robin in the eyes. "Did you kill George?"

"No! I would never— I wanted us to go to counseling. He promised not to hit me again, but that's what he did tonight. I left the room to think. I was coming back to insist on counseling, when there was an explosion. I came into the room and George was on the floor, bleeding. I grabbed the phone and called 911. Then I got a towel to stop the bleeding. The operator stayed on the line with me until the ambulance got there. But they said he was dead. They asked me about my gun. I told them I didn't have a gun."

"Is that true?"

"Yes! George had a gun, but he kept it locked in the closet."

"Did you tell the police that?"

"Yes. They got it."

"Okay. Wait here."

After talking to the arresting officers about fingerprints on the gun, which they'd taken and were awaiting results, she asked to take her client home.

"Ma'am, she hasn't been cleared of suspicion."

"Because you have an eyewitness?"

"No, but she is the only possible suspect."

"Were there windows in their apartment? Were they open?"

"Yes, but—"

"So, someone outside could've shot him, couldn't they?"

"It's possible, but—"

"Unless the fingerprints on the pistol in the apartment match my client's fingerprints, which I assume you've already taken, you have nothing to hold her on. It happened the way she said, and you can't prove differently."

The police sergeant stepped forward. "She can't be released until we've looked at the fingerprints found on the gun."

"Has the gun recently been fired?"

"Yes," one of the officers said.

"Did you ask my client if her husband had taken it to a shooting range in the past week?"

"She couldn't remember."

"How strange that her husband's death affected her memory." Lauren stared at the officer as if he were the guilty party.

The sergeant told one of the officers to go see about the prints on the gun.

"Good. I'll wait. In the meantime, I need a drink to take to my client. Do you have any Diet Cokes around here?"

"I'll get you one," one of the officers promised and left the area.

In a few minutes, Lauren returned to Robin's side with a Diet Coke. "Here, Robin, drink this." After Robin had a drink, Lauren said, "You told the officer you didn't know if George had taken the pistol to a shooting range. Does he usually do that?"

"Yes. He—he went out Tuesday to a gun range."

"Okay. Did you touch the gun at any time?"

"No, never. I don't like guns. Once he asked me to shoot it. That was when we were first married. I never touched it again."

"Good." Lauren nudged the Diet Coke a little closer. "Drink some more."

The door opened and an officer came in and told Lauren they had the results back.

"And?"

"Her prints aren't on the gun."

"So I assume you're not charging her."

"No, but don't plan any out-of-town trips," he told Robin in a gruff voice.

"No, she won't. Come on, Robin. We're going home."

"I—I can go?"

"Yes, I'm taking you to Reggie's apartment. I have a key."

"Is that her boyfriend?" the officer asked in a reasonable voice.

"No, it's my sister's apartment. Her name is Regina, but we call her Reggie." Lauren had read his mind knowing he was looking for a motive. Then she put an arm around Robin and walked her out of the police station.

"I should go home, but—but I don't think I can."

"No, you don't need to. I'll go back to your place and pack a bag for you after I get you settled."

In Lauren's car, Robin fell asleep. Lauren pulled out her cell phone. "Reggie, it's Lauren. Robin needs to stay with you a few days. I'm bringing her over."

"Why? Did she leave George?"

"Someone shot and killed George. The police thought it was her. I got her released and I'm bringing her to you. Then I'll go to her apartment and pack her some clothes so she doesn't have to go back there for a few days. Is that okay?"

"Sure. I've been telling her she needed to get out, but she kept giving him one more chance."

"You mean he's been abusing her?"

"Yeah. But I couldn't convince her to leave."

"Okay. We'll be there in about five minutes."

"Okay. Thanks, sis."

When she reached Reggie's second-floor

apartment near downtown, Lauren awakened Robin and led her upstairs.

"I—I don't know what to tell Reggie," Robin suddenly said as they reached the front door of Reggie's apartment.

"It's okay. I've already told her."

"Is it okay if I talk to her?"

"Yes, of course. But you can call me and talk if you need to."

"Thank you."

Once she'd turned Robin over to her sister, she went to Robin's apartment and showed her credentials to the policeman on duty. He oversaw her packing, to be sure she didn't remove any evidence. Then she took the bag back to Reggie's apartment.

She handed it to her sister since Robin was sleeping. Then she headed home. Once there, she called an investigator she used and asked him to check out some things about the deceased.

Lauren lay back and closed her eyes. That's when the picture of Ally in her new clothes hit her. She'd walked out on Jack and Ally. She picked up the phone again and dialed Jack's number.

"Jack, it's Lauren. I wanted to apologize for running out on you and Ally. Did you like her second outfit?"

"Yes, it was very nice."

He sounded stiff and unfriendly.

"I'm sorry about hurrying away, but it was an emergency, you know."

"No, I don't know. What kind of an emergency?"

"A client had been arrested, and I needed to get to her at once. They were trying to question her without me there. It was urgent that I be beside her."

"What had she done?"

"I can't talk about the case, Jack."

"And is this what happens whenever a client calls you?"

"It can. It's not usually this urgent, but it can be."

"Then I'm glad this happened. I don't want Ally connected to anyone who can walk out at a moment's notice."

"Now, just a minute, Jack. I was a lawyer before I met you two and I'll be a lawyer long after."

"I thought you weren't working for four weeks. But you forgot that rule the moment you got that call."

"Yes, I did. And that's my business. I left Ally with you. I knew she was safe. I didn't have time to do the niceties."

"I noticed."

"I won't bother you any longer, Jack." With that, she hung up the phone. Then she jumped to her feet and began pacing her bedroom floor. The gall of the man! She had done her job, left his daughter safely with him, and he was furious! How could he act like that? Did he think she should forget her job, her friend, and play with Ally?

She paced and worried for half an hour. As she did so, she relived another situation that had occurred in her life. A boyfriend had reacted much as Jack had, refusing to accept her apology for not meeting him because of an emergency. She'd called as soon as possible to let him know, but he'd told her she should've put him first. She'd thought they were serious, but he'd walked away, sure she'd come trailing after him.

She hadn't.

Was that what Jack thought, too? If so, she'd have to let him walk away. She had worked too hard and long to be where she was today. No man was worth giving up her career. Not even Jack Mason.

Chapter Nine

Jack wanted to refuse to return to his job in Lauren's apartment. He would prefer to be done with his association with the lady lawyer. But he never quit jobs. Never. So, on Monday morning, he dropped Ally off at the day care and headed to Lauren's apartment.

If she decided to fire him, of course, there wouldn't be any problem. He could walk away with a clear conscience. Or if she wanted him to finish the job, then that's what he would have to do.

Lauren opened the door to him and stood back for him to enter.

"Good morning."

"Good morning. How is Ally?"

"She's fine," he said and headed down the hallway to the back bedroom. He didn't intend to discuss his daughter with Lauren. There was no reason to do so. He didn't want Lauren to be a part of Ally's life.

Just as he entered the office, he looked back down the hall and saw Lauren still staring after him, as if he'd hurt her. Well, too bad. He wasn't going to risk Ally's heart just to please some big-time lawyer.

He worked all morning, striving to keep his mind off Lauren. Knowing she was just down the hall made his job that much more difficult.

There was a lot of phone activity, as if something was going on, but he told himself it had nothing to do with him. He was there to build cabinets and nothing more.

When lunchtime came, he only paused to say, "I'm going out for lunch. I need to buy some more supplies. I'll be back by two o'clock." That was a generous lunch, but he figured he was due an hour and then he'd go to the lumberyard and make some purchases.

She stared at him but said nothing, ignoring the plate of food she'd prepared for his lunch. After a minute, she turned her back on him.

Jack walked out of the apartment, wondering if he could stand the silent war that seemed to exist between them now. That he was responsible for initiating it didn't matter. He only hoped he survived it.

LAUREN HEARD the closure of the front door, meaning Jack had left the apartment. She'd hoped he would take the time to realize he'd misjudged her. But, obviously, that wasn't his take on their argument.

So she'd lost both Ally and Jack because she'd done her job. That wasn't fair, but as one of her law professors had often said, life wasn't fair.

She didn't feel like eating any lunch herself. She covered what she'd prepared and put it in the fridge. Just as she did so, the phone rang. Assuming it was the investigator with information, she hurried to answer it.

"Mrs. Mason? This is Mrs. Applebaum. I'm sorry to call, but Ally is sick and I can't reach her father. Can you come get her?"

"Yes, of course. What's wrong with her?"

"We're not sure, but she threw up and we don't want to take any chances. We felt sure you'd want to take her to her doctor."

"Yes, of course. I'll be right there."

Lauren grabbed a jacket and rushed out the

door. She was going to get to see Ally again. The only thing to rain on her parade was that Ally was ill. She wished she knew the name of the pediatrician Jack used. Maybe Ally would know.

When she reached the school and entered, Ally came flying down the hall into her arms. Lauren lifted the child against her, kissing her forehead to determine if Ally was feverish. She definitely was.

"Thank you for calling, Mrs. Applebaum."

"Well, I know her father wanted us to call him, but I didn't get any answer on his cell phone."

"Sometimes he forgets to turn it on. He'll be back this afternoon, so he'll know soon enough. In the meantime, I'll get her to the doctor."

"Good. I thought you would take care of everything."

"Yes, thank you. Do you have all your things, Ally?"

Ally nodded. Mrs. Applebaum handed over a pink backpack.

"It's all in here."

"Thank you, again."

Once she buckled Ally in her backseat, she asked, "Do you know your doctor's name?"

"It's Dr. Baker, but I don't want to go."

"But I'll be with you, sweetheart, and you have to go so we can get you well."

There were only two Bakers who were pediatricians. Lauren called the first one and got lucky. She took Ally to their nearby office. They put them in the sick child room to wait until they could get her in to see the doctor.

Half an hour later, Lauren carried Ally into the examining room.

The doctor entered and shook her hand. "I

didn't know Jack had married," he said with a big smile.

"He hasn't. I—I'm a friend and they couldn't reach Jack, so I brought Ally here."

"I see. Well, Ally, what's the matter?"

"My tummy doesn't feel good."

The doctor looked at the chart, noting the high fever. "When did you start feeling bad?"

"When I threw up."

"Not before? Did you feel hot earlier?"

"Yes. I told Daddy, but he said I was okay."

"Well, I need to listen to you breathe." He put his stethoscope against her chest and listened. "Okay. Now, can we take off your shirt for a minute?"

Ally nodded and Lauren helped her take off the yellow top she wore. The doctor looked at her chest, and lifted her arms to look at her armpits. Then he helped Ally put the top on again.

By then, Lauren wasn't surprised to discover the doctor's findings. She'd been through it a few times with her siblings.

"I'm afraid Ally has chicken pox. I'm surprised because I gave her the vaccine. It's a mild case, but she's definitely got the pox. She'll need to be kept down and get lots of rest until she feels better. Don't give her anything that will upset her stomach. She should be okay within a week. She can go back to school when she hasn't run fever for at least two days. Any questions?"

"No, I've been through this before," Lauren said with a smile.

"Ah. An experienced mother. Good. If you run into any problems, just give me a call."

"Yes, I will, thanks." Lauren lifted Ally into

her arms and carried her to the car. As she was buckling her into the backseat, Ally started crying.

"Don't cry, sweetie. It's okay."

"But I don't want to die!"

Lauren hugged the little girl. "You're not going to die. You're going to lie on my sofa and eat ice cream until you feel better. You'll be back at school next week."

"Really?" Ally asked, her voice wobbly as tears still spilled down on her cheeks.

"Absolutely. Your daddy is going to be quite surprised to find you with me when he comes back to work."

"Why wasn't Daddy there?"

"He had to go get some supplies. Now, no more questions until I get you on my sofa and turn on the television so you can watch your favorite shows."

In five minutes, they had reached Lauren's place and she spread a sheet on the sofa, along with several pillows, and had Ally under a blanket. *Sesame Street* was repeated several times a day and fortunately it was on now.

Lauren made a quick call to the preschool to warn them about a possible outbreak before she went to the kitchen to see what she had that Ally might want to eat. She scooped up a little ice cream in a cup and grabbed a spoon before she went back to the living room. When she got there, she discovered Ally had fallen asleep.

She sat beside the sick child, absentmindedly eating the ice cream before it melted, watching Ally sleep. It reminded her of taking care of her brothers and sisters when they'd been sick. She'd always worried that they might die, like her mother, and then her father, if she didn't take good care of them. She now knew that children seldom died from the illnesses, but she still wanted to give Ally the best care.

It was almost straight up two when she heard Jack coming in. She hurriedly got up from the couch and met him at the door.

"Jack, Ally's school tried to reach you, but you didn't have your cell phone on."

He frowned at her. "What's wrong?"

"Ally got sick."

"Where is she?"

"She's on my sofa. I picked her up and took her to the doctor."

"We use Dr. Baker. I'll take her to him."

"That's what I did. She's come down with the chicken pox. He thinks it's a mild case."

"But she had the vaccine!"

"That's what he said. She's asleep right now."

He glared at her and circled her to reach the

couch where his daughter lay. After staring at her, he reached out and stroked her cheek. Then he returned to Lauren's side.

"She's burning up."

"The doctor said to give her baby Tylenol. I gave her some as soon as we got home."

"But isn't there something else we can do?"

"Just keep her warm and comfortable."

"I should take her home."

"That's up to you, but she's happy where she is. When she wakes up, I'll let her eat ice cream and watch her television shows."

"You might get distracted!" he protested.

"I might, but I doubt it. If I do, I'll let you know, so you can stop work and take her home."

He walked back to Ally's side and stroked her cheek until she woke up.

"Hi, Daddy. I'm sick."

"I know, baby."

"But Lolly said I won't die. She said I can go back to school next week."

"That's right, if you stay down and rest."

"I will. See? Lolly made me a bed."

"Yes, I see, but I can take you home and take care of you until you're better."

"No. I want to stay here with Lolly. Please?"

"Okay, baby, but if you change your mind, just let me know."

"I will." She closed her eyes again, now that everything was settled to her liking.

Jack stood and faced Lauren.

"Thank you for taking care of Ally when I couldn't be there."

"I was glad to do so."

"I'll be in the office if she needs me."

Lauren watched his stiff back as he retreated to the office. She knew he hated having to depend on her for anything, but he would do so to make Ally happy. He was a good parent.

She went to the kitchen to make some oatmeal-raisin cookies. They would be good for Ally. It would give her something to munch on. And maybe her daddy, too.

Two hours later, when Ally woke up, Lauren fixed a tray for the little girl, putting the cookies and some milk on it. Then she added a cup of coffee. Before taking in the tray, she went down the hall.

Jack was concentrating on his work so hard, she called him several times to get his attention. "Ally is going to have a snack, and she'd like for you to join her."

She watched the mental debate that showed his struggle. Finally, he said, "Okay, I can take a break."

"Good. She's waiting for you." She went back down the hall, hoping he'd follow.

Ally smiled at her when she came into the living room, but Jack remained stone-faced.

"If you need anything else, I'll be in the kitchen," Lauren said. She knew Jack wouldn't talk to his daughter until she was out of the room.

"Where are you going?" Ally asked.

"I'm making some more cookies so we'll have plenty while you're getting better."

"But I—"

"Let Lauren go to the kitchen, baby. She has a lot to do."

Lauren wanted to return to the sofa and argue with him. She knew he wanted her to go to the kitchen so he wouldn't have to talk to her. Fine! That was what she intended to do anyway.

She baked more cookies and occupied

herself in other ways until Jack appeared in the doorway, carrying the tray.

"I appreciate your including me in Ally's tea party."

"No problem." She took the tray from him.

"No, I didn't deserve— I was just trying to protect Ally. She has trouble understanding why she doesn't have a mother when other girls do. Her mother's desertion occurred when she was an infant, so it doesn't hurt her so badly. But if a new mother deserted her, whatever the reason, it would hurt so much more."

Lauren stared at him. "I understand."

Then she turned her back on him and began washing the dishes.

"Lauren, maybe I was a little harsh the other day. But I can't—"

"I said I understand, Jack. But leaving her with you because I had an emergency is not abandoning her. Just as you didn't abandon her today by forgetting to have your cell phone on. I filled in for you today, just as you filled in for me on Saturday."

He stared at her for a few seconds. Then he turned and went down the hallway.

Lauren was disappointed but not surprised. She knew how protective Jack was of his little girl. But if she had the choice, she still would've gone to Robin's aid.

With a sigh, she wiped down the tray and stored it away. Then she went in to check on Ally. She was back asleep, but her hair was damp and she'd pushed off the blanket. Lauren covered her with a sheet and let her continue to sleep.

Taking a legal pad, she outlined her options for Robin's case. The investigator she used had come up with several different angles. It appeared that Robin's husband had led a different life from what his wife had known about. Her investigator, Mike, had suggested he look into the gambling and prostitution connections and get back to her with details.

In the meantime, she needed Robin's permission to look at their financial records to see how George had covered his activities. She reached for the phone just as she heard Ally wake up. She immediately hung up the phone and moved to the little girl's side.

"Hi, Ally. How are you feeling?"

"I'm thirsty," Ally mumbled.

"I'll get you some juice. That will make you feel better."

"And more cookies?"

"Hmm, I suppose a few more."

"Daddy ate most of the cookies earlier," Ally said hurriedly.

"Oh, he did, did he? I'll have to talk to him about that."

"Maybe I ate some, too, but one or two more wouldn't hurt me, would it?"

"No, of course not," Lauren said, bending over to kiss Ally's forehead. "Do you need a trip to the bathroom while I get you another snack?"

"Yes, please," Ally agreed, slipping off the sofa.

When Ally was tucked up again on the sofa, Lauren served her patient some juice and several more cookies.

"I love you, Lolly," Ally said as Lauren sat beside her.

"I love you, too, sweetheart," Lauren said with a smile.

"Why does Daddy get upset?"

Lauren paused before she said, "Your

daddy is afraid you'll think I'm your mommy, and I'm not."

"I know. You would have to live with us for you to be my mommy. That happened to Mindy, only different. Her daddy moved out and now he's not her daddy anymore."

"Yes, he is, sweetie. He will always be Mindy's daddy."

"No. He has to live with them to be her daddy. Mindy said."

Lauren didn't want to upset her, so she didn't argue the point. "Well, your daddy doesn't want you to think that I'm your mommy. I'll try to be a friend, because I care about you, but that doesn't mean I'll always be there for you."

"You mean like on Saturday?"

"Yes. I wouldn't have left you alone if your daddy hadn't been there. I would've taken you with me. But I still had to go help my friend."

"Where did you go?"

"To the police station."

"Wow! That would've been exciting!"

"Ally!" Both females jumped when Jack's voice interrupted them. "What are you talking about?"

"Going with Lolly on Saturday. She went to the police station. I've never been there."

"And you're not going there, either," Jack said forcefully.

"You make it sound like that would be a terrible thing, Jack," Lauren protested. "She would've been safe."

"I don't want my child going to the police station. There's no telling what she would've seen."

Lauren rolled her eyes at Jack, but she said nothing. She didn't want to upset Ally. "Is there something wrong? Why are you in here?"

"Because it's time for me to stop work. Is that okay with you?" he demanded.

Lauren looked at her watch, amazed that time had passed so quickly. "Of course. I hadn't realized the time. You'll bring Ally back tomorrow, won't you?"

"No. I think the two of us will stay home tomorrow and give her a chance to rest."

"But, Daddy—" Ally started to protest.

"No, Ally. No arguing!" he said sharply.

When the child looked at Lauren, her eyes large with emotion, Lauren reached out to pat the little girl's arm. "It's all right, Ally. Maybe if you're a good girl, Daddy will bring you back the next day. How about I go pack up some cookies for you to take home with you?"

Ally nodded.

"Good. I'll be right back."

After Lauren had left the room, the child

looked at her father. "I know she's not my mommy, but I love her. Why can't I come tomorrow?"

"Because it's not good for you to get too involved with a lawyer."

"Why? What's wrong with a lawyer? And what about Lolly?"

"Baby, Lauren is a lawyer. And a lawyer works long hours. She doesn't have time to spend with you."

"But she does. We made cookies!"

"I know, but she'll be going back to work in a week. Then she won't have time for you. So it's better that you don't get used to it now."

"Jack Mason, how dare you! That's nonsense and you know it!"

At the sound of Lauren's voice, coming from over his shoulder, Jack spun around.

Lauren stood there glaring at him, her

hands squeezing the container of cookies, her eyes flashing fire. The flames were aimed right at him.

Chapter Ten

Jack accepted the challenge and stood his ground. "I'm not trying to insult you, Lauren. I'm just being realistic." He crossed his arms over his chest. "I've dated a lawyer before."

"Sometimes lawyers do work long hours. But let me ask you this. How much more time do you spend with her? After all, you usually leave her at school in the morning and pick her up in the evening."

"I'm there for her in the evenings!" Jack responded.

"I know. But you make it sound like you spend all day with your daughter." She pointed her finger at him to emphasize her remark. "In fact, *you* spend the same amount of time that any working parent does."

"So, you're not a working parent."

"No, I'm not and I'm not asking to be. I'm asking to be Ally's friend. I want to spend time with her on Saturdays or Sunday afternoons, which would give you a little break from being a parent 24/7."

"I don't mind it."

"I didn't say you complained, but a little free time wouldn't hurt."

"I'm going to have some free time." His voice sounded calmer now as he explained, "My mother called last night. She and Dad have decided to drive to Dallas to spend a week with me and Ally. They haven't seen her since she was a baby."

Lauren let her anger fade, too, turning her attention to Ally now. "How nice! Won't that be fun, Ally? Getting to know your grandparents?"

"I guess so," Ally said, still lying down on the sofa. "Will they come to see Lolly, too?" she asked her father.

"No, sweetheart," Jack hurriedly said. "You'll get to stay home with them. You won't have to go to school."

"But, Daddy, I'm learning my letters. I can't miss school."

"Well, you have to miss school while you're sick. But you can catch up when you go back to school. And you'll get more rest, staying at home with Grandma and Grandpa."

"Will they like that?"

"Sure they will. And maybe, after you get well, they can take you to the zoo. That would be fun, wouldn't it?"

"And Lolly could go with us!" Ally beamed at Lauren.

"She doesn't want to go to the zoo," Jack interjected.

"I think I'd like it," Lauren said with a smile at the little girl. "In fact…" She paused and looked at Jack. "When will your parents get here?"

"They're driving. They should get here Friday afternoon. They didn't want to hurry."

"Why don't you all come to dinner on Saturday evening?"

"Yay!" Ally cried in agreement.

Jack shook his head. "I don't think they'd be comfortable. They don't know you."

"Daddy, they'll love Lolly! I know they would."

Lauren thanked the girl, then said to Jack, "You can let me know after you talk to your parents. In the meantime, I think you should bring Ally here again tomorrow. She's comfortable here, and she can see you when she feels like it."

"We'll see," Jack muttered as Ally pleaded to come to Lauren's the next day. He stood and scooped his daughter up in his arms. "I'll take her out to the car."

"Shall I bring the cookies?"

"Yes, please," he agreed.

She hoped that meant he liked the cookies, too. Not that he'd admit it, of course. He seemed to think denial made him strong.

She saw them off, waving to Ally. Then she returned to her apartment. Though she intended to do some work on Robin's case, she first walked to her future study to look at the work Jack had been doing. It was remarkable, as Judge Robinson had promised. Jack was transforming the room into a highly functional work space.

She had mixed feelings about his finishing the work next week. She wanted to have her new office, but she would miss both Jack and Ally. She'd fallen in love with Ally....

And maybe a little with Jack, too, added an inner voice.

But he'd made it clear that she wouldn't qualify for Ally's mommy, because she was a lawyer.

After a struggle, she put away those thoughts and turned to Robin's case. She had to prepare a defense for Robin in case the police decided to charge her. So far, they still considered Robin their only suspect.

Who had killed George? she asked herself.

George was providing her with ample possibilities. He was a gambler and promiscuous.

He frequented Dallas's red-light district, according to her investigator. However, though he'd tried talking to the working women, they were unwilling to admit anything, fearing he was an undercover cop.

She thought she'd wait until Friday night and go talk to the women herself. Maybe they would identify George and tell her about problems with the man.

She was a little uneasy about venturing into that area of Dallas, but she had to find out what she could about George. For Robin.

As she jotted down possible questions, the telephone rang.

"Hello?"

"Hi, Lauren, it's Jack. I wanted to apologize for not appreciating your fast action in picking up Ally and getting her to the doctor."

"That's all right, Jack."

"No. It's my fault that I didn't have my phone on."

"I didn't mind. But I wish you'd bring her over tomorrow."

"She wants to come, but I think it would be better if we stayed home and collected ourselves. Life's been changing too quickly and we need to adjust."

"All right, but if you change your mind, I'll be here."

"I really appreciate your offer, but—but we're going to stay home."

After Jack hung up the phone, Lauren sat against the back of her bed, thinking about the gruff man who wanted to protect his little girl from hurt. Ally was a lucky little girl.

She wished she could share in that luck.

AT TEN THE NEXT MORNING, a knock sounded on Lauren's door. When she swung the door open, she discovered Jack with Ally in his arms. Her face was buried against her daddy's neck and he held her close.

"Is she all right?" Lauren asked, worry in her voice.

"She's been crying to come over here. I finally gave in." Jack pulled away from his child. "Do you hear me, Ally? We're at Lauren's house, so you can quit hiding."

The little girl moved so swiftly that she took both adults by surprise by diving into Lauren's arms.

"Oh, my, I'm glad you came to see me, Ally. Would you like to lie on the sofa and watch television?"

Her head bobbed up and down, but she didn't speak.

"All right, sweetheart. Let's get a sheet and blanket and put you on the sofa. Can Daddy hold you while I get the bedding?"

Ally went back to her father, but she didn't feel very good, so she snuggled against him.

"I think she's running a fever again. I brought the baby Tylenol with us in case she needed it," Jack called.

"Good. Why don't you put her on the sofa and go get some water from the kitchen."

Jack did as Lauren suggested. By the time he got back from the kitchen, a glass of water in his hand, Lauren had the bed made up on the sofa with Ally tucked up under the blanket. She took the medicine from her daddy and the water and swallowed it.

"Lolly, stay here with me," Ally whispered, clutching Lauren's hand.

"Of course, sweetie. Look, I've turned on *Clifford the Big Red Dog*."

Ally shifted her gaze to the television. It

only took a couple of minutes, now that she'd settled down, to fall asleep.

When her breathing evened and deepened, Jack stood. "Thanks, Lauren. I couldn't quiet her down this morning."

"I'm glad you brought her, Jack."

"I'll go get busy on your office."

"Thank you." She watched Jack straighten his broad shoulders and walk down the hall as if he were setting out to conquer the world. Her world.

She sat beside Ally for another five minutes, enjoying the peace she felt at having both of them back in her apartment.

AT LUNCH TIME, when Jack entered the kitchen, he found his daughter sipping some tomato soup, a thick roast beef sandwich at his place, and Lauren smiling at him. He thought the latter was the perfect touch, no matter what he was eating.

Then he frowned. That wasn't what he should be feeling. He would only be working here through next week. Then he'd move on to another job. A job where he brought his own lunch every day and ate alone. Normal.

Normal was how life should be, he decided. And lunch with Lauren wasn't normal. She could sway his mood in seconds. No wonder she was so good with a jury.

"Is something wrong with your sandwich, Jack?" Lauren asked.

He jerked his head up. "No, it's great."

"You were frowning so much, I thought maybe you didn't like it."

"I like it." He smoothed out his brow and

continued eating. Beside him, Ally was drooping. "Are you all right, baby?" he asked.

"I'm not so hungry, Lolly," Ally said. "I think I want to go back to my bed."

"I'll carry her," Jack insisted, standing to pick her up.

"Of course. I'll go straighten her cover for her."

Once they got Ally settled on the sofa, Jack stood staring at his child. "Do you think we should call the doctor?"

"No, she's doing fine. The first few days are the worst. In a couple of days we'll have trouble keeping her down."

Jack took her word for it. He went back down the hall, wishing Lauren could always be around, be there for Ally, for him. His mother had been a stay-at-home mom, and he'd always thought he wanted that kind of mother for his children.

But maybe he could have a wife who worked a little. But a lawyer? A lawyer didn't know what working a little was about. A lawyer didn't believe in coming home before midnight. At least that was what he'd seen when he dated a lawyer. Definitely not for him and Ally.

THE REST OF THE WEEK, Jack brought Ally to work with him at Lauren's. Each day Lauren would take Ally to the sofa and make sure she was warm and happy.

On Friday, Lauren answered the phone about one-thirty, while Ally was sleeping. The caller was Jack's mother.

"Hello, Mrs. Mason. I'm Lauren McNabb. Jack is building my study for me." Apparently the Masons had arrived in Dallas. "Would you like to come here? Or I can tell Jack to stop work and send him and Ally home."

"If you don't mind, we'll come over there," Mrs. Mason replied. "We don't want to interfere with Jack's work, but we're anxious to meet Ally."

"Of course, here are the directions."

After she got off the phone, she straightened up her living room a little and made a pitcher of iced tea. After that, she stepped back to her office.

As usual, Jack was concentrating on his work. Lauren had to tap him on his shoulder, and he jumped as if she'd stuck a gun in his ribs. He moved so fast, he threw Lauren off balance. She was on the verge of falling, when he caught her against him.

"Are you all right?" he asked, staring down at her.

"I—I'm fine," Lauren assured him. "I came to tell you your parents are here."

Not realizing he was still holding her, Jack couldn't believe her words. "What are they doing here? They don't even known where you live."

"I didn't mean they were *here*. At least not yet. They're in town, and I invited them here. I thought it would be nice if they met Ally here. She'll be more relaxed."

"Why would she be more relaxed here?"

"Because I'm here with her, even though you're working. They may be her grandparents, but she doesn't remember them." She pushed against his chest. "Jack, I'm fine. You can turn me loose."

"Oh. Yeah." He dropped his arms and noticed how empty they felt after holding Lauren. "Okay, so they're coming here?"

"Yes. You can show them your work. They'll be very proud."

"Yeah, sure. Is Ally awake?"

"Not yet. I thought she should sleep as much as she can."

"Yeah, but she's all right?"

"Yes, of course. She's getting better every day. I think she'll be able to go to school next week."

"We'll see."

They both heard the doorbell ring. Jack put down his tools and followed Lauren to the door.

When his parents entered, they hugged Jack and told him how happy they were to see him. But his mother was peeking over his shoulder, looking for her grandchild.

"She's still sleeping, Mrs. Mason," Lauren said quietly. "We'll wake her up now. Come with me."

They moved into the living room where Ally was sleeping on the sofa.

"Oh, isn't she sweet," Jack's mother whispered, tears in her eyes.

"Why don't you go look at the work Jack is doing. I'll have some refreshments ready when you come back in and Ally will be awake then."

Jack led his parents down the hall to where he'd been working.

"Jack, I like your friend. She's lovely," Carol Mason told him the moment they were out of earshot.

Jack jerked around just before they entered the study. "She's my boss, Mom. That's all."

"Oh, you're not dating?"

"No! Don't even suggest such a thing." Then he took them into the study. "I've been working here three weeks. I should finish the job next week."

"Oh, Jack, this is lovely," Carol said. Turning to her husband, she said, "Jim, have you ever seen such exquisite work?"

"You're doing a good job, son. Is there a lot of demand for this work? Are you making enough to support you and Ally?"

"Yeah, Dad, and I still have a lot of money from when I sold my company. We're doing fine."

"Good. I'm glad to hear it."

"We worry about you, Jack, here by yourself with the baby. We've been thinking we were pretty selfish, taking off for Florida, leaving you here on your own," Carol confessed.

"Not now, Carol," Jim Mason told his wife. "We'll talk about it later."

"Come on. Lauren wants to give you iced tea and cookies."

Jack led the way back to the living room.

Ally was just waking up. Lauren took her in her arms and introduced her to her grandparents.

Leaning her head against Lauren's shoulder, Ally smiled shyly at her grandparents.

"Please, sit down. Ally and I will go bring in the refreshments."

After Lauren and Ally had left the room, Carol said, "They seem very close."

"Too close. She's a lawyer. She doesn't have time for children."

"But she's here with Ally today."

"Yes, Mom, because she's off work for a month. After next week, she'll go back to work. I've dated lawyers before. They work ridiculous hours."

"I think that's what you used to work, too," Jim said. "We never got to see you. That's one of the reasons we moved away. We decided we couldn't build our lives around you. You were busy and I thought you were happy."

"I thought I was, too, but Ally has turned my life around. I know what's important now."

"That's good," Carol agreed. "And she's so pretty. She looks like you, Jack."

"Yeah. And she's just as stubborn."

Carol couldn't hold back a smile.

"I'll apologize now for the headaches I gave you. But even so, Ally is worth a few headaches."

Carol laughed, and Jim grinned.

Lauren came into the living room, carrying a tray with glasses of iced tea, and Ally carried a plate with cookies.

"My, my, look how well Ally is helping," Carol said.

"She's a big help," Lauren said. "Sometimes she helps me make cookies. Not today, because

she's been sick, but she's almost well now."
Lauren served everyone the iced tea, and Ally,
at Lauren's encouragement, carried the tray
around so everyone could get some cookies.

Ally even giggled when her grandfather
teased her about taking all the cookies.

"Oh, we've missed so much already," Carol
said softly.

"But you have so much more to look
forward to," Lauren told her.

"Yes." Then she looked at Lauren. "You
sound a great deal like a woman who has
raised children."

"I have raised children. My mother died
when I was twelve and I helped raise my
brothers and sisters."

"How many do you have?" Carol asked,
sympathy in her eyes.

"I have four brothers and twin sisters."

"My, that must have made your life difficult."

"Yes, but I wouldn't trade that experience for the world."

"I think Jack is finding it well worthwhile, also."

"I think it's nice that you and your husband can come visit them. I would like to have you over here for dinner tomorrow night, if you don't think you'll be too tired to come."

"I think that's a lovely idea. Jim, Lauren is inviting us to dinner tomorrow night. Isn't that wonderful?"

"Why, that's very neighborly of you, Lauren. We'd love to come, right, Ally?"

Ally giggled again. "Yes, Grandpa."

Jim beamed at the little girl. "I like hearing you call me Grandpa in person. That's perfect."

"You call me Grandma, right, Ally?"

"Yes, that's what Daddy said."

"And Daddy is right," Carol said with a big smile. "Oh, it's going to be so much fun. Maybe we can go shopping one day. I need to buy you some pretty things."

"And Lolly can go with us," Ally agreed.

Carol looked confused. "Who is Lolly?"

"That's what she calls me, Mrs. Mason. Lauren is a hard name to say, so she calls me Lolly."

"I think it would be nice if Lauren could join us."

"Ally, your Grandma might like to have you to herself," Lauren said gently.

"No, dear, I don't know where to go. I'd love to have you join us."

"We'll talk about it tomorrow evening. Ally and I have been shopping once together. It was a lot of fun, wasn't it, Ally?"

"Yeah, lots!" Ally said with a big smile.

"Oh, good. Then Lauren will know where we should shop."

"I think you may be too tired for dinner tomorrow, Mom," Jack interjected with a frown.

"Nonsense. We stopped yesterday at Shreveport and gambled a little at one of the casinos. Then we slept in this morning, had a lovely breakfast and drove here this afternoon. That's not too much of a drain. Do you go to Shreveport to gamble, Lauren?"

"No, I've never done that."

"It's relaxing for a little while, but I'm afraid I get bored with it after a while," Carol said.

"My brothers went there for the weekend once, but they felt the same way."

"It is so wonderful that you have such a big family," Carol said. "Your dad must be so proud."

"He was, but he's gone now. He died when I was nineteen."

"Oh, I'm sorry, dear."

"It's all right. My siblings and I have each other."

"Jack is my only child. I had several miscarriages after him, and the doctor didn't think we should try again."

"That's so hard," Lauren said. "But I guess we can't determine what will happen in our lives."

"True. Look at Jack. He didn't plan on Ally, but—well, he made the right decision when he learned about her."

"Yes, he's done an amazing job."

Carol beamed at Lauren. She seemed perfect to Carol…for her son.

Chapter Eleven

Carol dropped more than a few hints for her son about choosing Lauren to be a part of his life. By Saturday night he finally lost his temper.

"Mom! I told you she's a lawyer! She's home now because she burned out working nonstop, until her boss sent her home."

"But people change, dear. She might not work as much if she had a family."

"She's already raised a family, Mom. She told you. That's why she's not interested in having a family."

"I didn't hear her say that. Did you, Jim?" she asked her husband when he entered the living room ready for dinner at Lauren's. "Did you hear her say she didn't want a family?"

"No, Carol, but you don't need to organize Jack's life. He's doing all right on his own."

"But Lauren is such a sweet young woman."

"Carol," Jim said in a warning tone. "Enough."

Jack thanked his father after his mother had left the room.

"I'm not saying your mother is wrong, son. But it's your choice. If the young lady doesn't interest you…"

Jack stalked out of the room.

A few minutes later, when they were gathered to drive to Lauren's, Carol smiled at Ally. "You look lovely, Ally. That's a pretty dress."

"Thank you. Lolly picked it out."

"Well, she certainly has lovely taste. How is she as a cook?" Carol asked, looking at her son.

"She's a good cook, Mom." Jack held open the door for everyone to go outside to his car.

"Oh, I love this fall weather. We don't have a fall down in Florida. It's always hot."

"I know some people who would trade with you come January," Jack told her.

"Oh, you don't have bad winters here in Dallas. It's not like you live in North Dakota."

"No, but it can get chilly in January and February. I thought you moved to Florida because you liked warm weather."

"She's changed her mind," Jim said.

Jack looked over his shoulder at his mother in the backseat. "Are you thinking about returning to Texas?"

"Well, your father and I have talked about it. Jim doesn't like to play as much golf as the other men. He could play enough golf here in Dallas. And I miss you and Ally, and my friends."

"But you haven't been down there five years yet."

"I know, but you've only been down to see us once. We thought you'd come down more often."

"Mom, it's more difficult when you have a baby."

"I know, dear, and if we'd known about Ally before we moved, we wouldn't have done so."

"Your mother has worried a lot about you handling Ally on your own," Jim muttered under his breath.

Jack didn't say anything else before they got to Lauren's place.

Lauren greeted them warmly, inviting them in.

After they were seated, she brought out some hors d'oeuvres and offered them to everyone.

Carol raved about the hot cheesy toasts. "I need to get your recipe. My group of friends love hot hors d'oeuvres."

"Oh, really? In Florida, I guess I thought everyone served cold hors d'oeuvres."

"Oh, that's true in Florida. But Jim and I have been thinking about moving back to Dallas. We miss our friends, and we want to be here to see Ally grow up. When we left, we seldom saw Jack. And he didn't give any indication that he would be settling down. We were so surprised when he told us about Ally."

"I can imagine. But I'm sure you'd enjoy being around for Ally. Grandparents are important in a child's life."

"Yes, I think so, too."

The conversation turned general until Lauren got up to go to the kitchen, Carol following to help.

Jim leaned over and took another hors d'oeuvre. "These are mighty tasty."

"Yes, she's a good cook."

"And a nice lady."

"Yeah."

"A real beauty."

"You're beginning to sound like Mom."

"Sorry." After a minute, Jim said, "Will our moving back mess things up for you?"

"Heck, no, Dad. I could've used you here three weeks ago when they closed Ally's child care center. I intend to keep her in the school she's in, but when she's sick, it would be nice to have some backup."

"Good. Your mom has been making this decision for the past six months. You know how she worries over a bone for a long time before she takes a bite."

"Yeah, I know. But will you be happy back here in Dallas?"

"Sure. I was happy before we moved. She felt we were missing out on life in Florida."

"Gentlemen, and Ally, of course," Lauren said from the dining room door. "Dinner is served."

AFTER AN ENJOYABLE DINNER, Carol suggested they leave and Lauren said how much she'd enjoyed getting to know them. Both Jim and Jack thanked her for dinner. She was seeing them to the door when the phone rang.

She excused herself and went to answer it. Jack couldn't help but overhear her end of the conversation.

"Now? I suppose I could. You're sure? Okay, I'll try again tonight."

She hung up the phone and returned to the door.

"What was that? A problem?" Jack demanded.

"No, of course not." He continued to stare at her and she said, "Not exactly. I just hadn't planned on— Nothing. I'll be fine."

"Where are you going?"

Carol admonished her son. "Jack, I don't think you should ask."

"It's all right, Carol," Lauren said. "It's just some research I need to do. I tried last night, but my investigator thinks I should go tonight."

"Where are you going?" Jack asked again.

"Near downtown."

"Who's going with you?"

"Jack, I'm a big girl. I can go out on my own."

Jack tossed his keys to his father. "Dad, can you get Mom and Ally home? I'll stay and go with Lauren. She'll bring me home when whatever she has to do is over."

"Jack, you're not going to like this," Lauren protested, as he closed the door after his parents and daughter.

"Why not?" he asked.

"Because I need to go talk to some prostitutes."

LAUREN DIDN'T WANT to admit that she'd been worried about going alone to the seedy area of downtown Dallas. But now that Jack was with her, she felt a great deal braver.

Once she'd explained the situation to Jack, she wasn't surprised he'd insisted on accompanying her. Her investigator had struck out with the prostitutes, who'd refused to answer his questions, thinking he was a cop. Her only hope was to talk to the women herself.

Jack was not at all happy with her plans. Ever since they'd got into the car, he had advised her against it.

"How do you even intend to meet these ladies?" he asked her now.

"I'm going to get out of the car at certain street corners and interview them."

"Do you think they'll talk to you?"

"I think so."

"And what do I do?"

"I'd like you to drive the car and follow me along, staying close."

"Are you taking a weapon?"

"A weapon?" Lauren asked, staring at him.

"A gun. Do you have a gun?"

"No, I don't. And I don't need one. There's practically a policeman on every corner."

"If that were true, there wouldn't be such a big business."

"How do you know?"

"I read the newspapers and watch the news on television."

She didn't bother to argue, passing the rest of the ride in silence.

It was a fifteen-minute drive but the neighborhood changed drastically. In spite of her comment about police presence, they found an area where no police could be seen. There was a collection of ladies on the corners, dressed in cheap clothes and wearing heavy makeup. Jack pulled to the curb, and Lauren slipped out of the car.

"Hello, ladies," she said as she approached them. "I'm a defense attorney looking for information about the man my client is accused of killing. I was told he visited you ladies frequently. Could you look at the picture?"

Most of the women moved away, but several of them stopped to look at the picture.

"Oh, that's George," one of them said, and began to turn away.

"Wait! You know who he is? Did he do business with you?"

"Only once. After that I wouldn't have anything to do with him, no matter how poor I was that night."

"Why not?" Lauren asked.

"He's a beater. I had a black eye just 'cause he didn't want to pay me. And I did exactly what he asked for."

"Did you see him around here often?"

"Yeah. All the time. I warned the young ones to stay away from him. Then Ceci died. I know he killed her, but the police didn't think so."

"Ceci who?"

"I don't know. We just called her Ceci."

"What year was that?"

"Two, maybe three years ago."

Lauren couldn't get any more information from her, so she moved down the street, looking for another lady of the night who might recognize George.

It was comforting to see Jack following her in her car.

"HEY, BIG BOY. You interested in a little fun?"

Jack stared at the woman leaning into the passenger window. "Uh, no, thank you. I'm here with a friend."

"Oh, really? What's your friend interested in?"

"She's trying to get some information about a man."

"She? Your friend is a she?"

"Yeah."

"Are you sure?"

"Yes, I'm sure. I'm not interested."

He had to repeat that conversation on every corner where Lauren was interviewing. When she finally returned to the car for the last time, he breathed a sigh of relief.

"How'd it go?" he asked.

"All right. I appreciate your coming with me tonight. It would've taken a lot longer if I'd had to park my car every block I went to."

"I'm glad I could be of some help. Ready to go home now?"

"Yes, please."

"Do you do this kind of thing often?"

"No, I never have before. But I have to find an alternative in case they charge her. The police haven't come to a decision."

"Do you think she did it?"

"Absolutely not."

"How do you know?"

"I know Robin. She was still convinced George would change if he'd just go to counseling."

"Maybe she was right."

"No. He was a wife beater. And according to these women tonight, he may have done even worse."

"What are you talking about?"

"To a woman, they all believe he killed a working lady a couple of years ago. I've got to look into that case."

"Just because he hit his wife occasionally doesn't make him a killer," Jack said with a frown.

"Eventually it will. It's an illness that grows. It starts out with an occasional hit for what he thinks is a good reason. Then he keeps hitting, always apologizing afterward and swearing never to do it again."

"Maybe he means it."

"No. Have you ever hit a woman?"

"No, of course not!"

"Why not?"

"Because I'm bigger and stronger than most women. I don't beat men, either."

"Good. I just thought I should ask. You were defending that kind of behavior."

"Men get abused as much as women. You know that, don't you?" Jack asked.

"Yes, I've had that kind of case before."

"Were you on the man's side or the woman's?"

"The man's side. I don't believe anyone should be beaten, regardless of what's wrong. That's not the way to fix anything."

"I agree." He pulled her car to a stop in

front of his house. "Thanks for an interesting evening."

"Probably not what you expected." Lauren opened her door and got out to come around to the driver's side.

Jack got out and stood waiting for her to reach him. When she did so, he stepped backward to give her room, but she tripped on the curb and pitched forward into his arms.

"Oh! I'm sorry. I didn't mean—"

Her apology was silenced as Jack bent and covered her lips with his.

Shock was fleeting. All she could feel was his mouth on hers. The man was an incredible kisser. And she met his kiss with enthusiasm.

When he finally pulled away, he muttered, "This would all be easier if you weren't such a great kisser."

"You're no slouch, yourself," she returned. Though she would've like to stay and step into his arms again, instead she slipped into the driver's seat.

"Call me when you get home," Jack told her. "So I'll know you're in safe and sound."

"I'll be fine."

"And I'll be waiting to hear from you."

She didn't make him wait too long. As soon as she got home, she walked to the phone and dialed Jack's number.

Jack picked up on the first ring. "Are you inside your apartment?"

"Yes, I am."

"Did you lock the front door?"

"Of course I did, Jack. I'm not an idiot."

"I just wanted to be sure you're safe. You didn't give any of those ladies your address, did you?"

"Only my office address."

"But you're not at your office."

"But I will be in a week. And I can call them back if they call in."

"All right, but don't arrange to meet them anywhere alone," Jack warned. "If you're going to meet one of them, I'll come with you."

"Jack, I'm a big girl. I can manage on my own."

"No. Just give me a call."

"I'll see."

"All right. Good night."

Lauren hung up the phone, shaking her head. She didn't know what was going on with Jack. One minute he kissed her like he'd never let her go. Then he assured her she wouldn't be a good mother for Ally. One minute he wanted her to lock up and not take chances, as if her welfare mattered to him.

Then he couldn't wait until he finished her job and walked out of her life.

She was thoroughly confused.

JACK'S MOTHER was waiting for him when he hung up the phone. "Did you have a nice evening with Lauren?" she asked.

"It was business, Mom. She was doing research for a case she's handling. I didn't think she should go on her own."

"That's very gentlemanly of you, dear," Carol said. "And she's such a nice young lady."

"Yes, she is. And a well-known lawyer. Too bad she's not the motherly type."

"Ally seems to think so." Carol watched her son closely.

"Mom, I'd love for you and Dad to move back to Dallas, but I'm not looking for a match-maker. Ally and I are a family all by ourselves."

"But don't you want other children? It's hard to have only one. We know, don't we, Jim?"

"Yes, dear, we do. But we did a good job with Jack, and he'll do a good job with Ally. She's a beautiful little girl. Very bright."

"Thanks, Dad. I think so, too."

Carol crossed her arms over her chest. "I think you're being selfish. It's not fair to stay away from Lauren just because she's a lawyer."

"If I'm going to find a mother for Ally, I need a woman who isn't dedicated to her work. You know that, Mom. You were always home when I got home from school. That would never happen with Lauren."

"That was a different time, son. Nowadays, women don't sit around waiting for a man to come along and marry them. I got married when I was nineteen. I was working as a shop girl. It wasn't exactly a career."

"That's true, Mom, but I want Ally to have that kind of support."

"And will you want her to avoid a career because she might not make a good wife?" Carol asked.

"Of course not. I want her to do what she enjoys doing."

"So why is it so unreasonable of Lauren to have that?"

Jack looked at his mother, but did not reply. He was thoroughly confused.

Chapter Twelve

On Sunday afternoon all of Lauren's family came over for dinner, except Steve, who was still away for military training. James brought Cheryl and Reggie brought Robin with her.

"Jack and Ally aren't here?" Bill asked after he came in.

"No, they're not."

"I wanted to meet him," Reggie said.

"Who are we talking about?" Ginny asked.

"Lauren's boyfriend," Reggie said casually.

"What? Why didn't anyone tell me? What's he like?"

"I've heard he's a hunk. Bill, Barry and James have met him."

Lauren was in the kitchen, putting the last touches on the meal, and appeared at the door of the living room to call them all to the table. She was met with questions about Jack and Ally.

"We can talk about that later. Come to the table."

"But, Lauren, everyone else knows except me," Ginny complained.

"Ginny, there's nothing to tell. I'll explain after we start eating."

Instead of silencing the questions, the others began demanding to know what had happened.

She sat down at the table and remained silent until they joined her. Then she asked the blessing. Finally, she said, "Jack and I are not dating. He's working on my study. That's all."

"But we went to the baseball game with you," Barry pointed out.

"Yes, I know. But we aren't dating."

"It sure looked like it that night," Bill said.

Lauren drew a deep breath. "I'm telling you we are not dating. He's building my office for me. That's all."

"What about Ally?" James asked. "She seemed to think you were applying to be her mother."

"That was a misunderstanding. Her father hates lawyers."

"Jack? Jack hates lawyers? Didn't you tell him you're a lawyer?" Barry asked.

"Yes, he knew that when he began working here."

"Then I don't understand."

Lauren sighed. "There's nothing to understand."

"You mean it's over even before I found out about it?" Ginny lamented. "That's so unfair!"

Lauren filled her plate and began to eat, unwilling to say anything else.

Finally the rest of them did the same. Conversation turned general and Lauren relaxed slightly, but she didn't breathe a sigh of relief until after her family had departed.

"Great! Now he makes me uncomfortable with my own family!"

She hadn't even reached the sofa when someone knocked on her door. Assuming one of the family had left something behind, she swung the door wide, only to come face-to-face with Jack and her entire family.

"Look who we found in the parking lot," Bill pointed out, a big grin on his face. "We introduced Ginny and Reggie to him."

"That's good. Did you introduce Robin also?"

"Oh, yeah, we did," Barry said.

"Fine. Now, are you all coming back in, or going home?" Lauren asked in exasperation.

"Oh, we're all going home," Reggie said cheerfully. "We don't want to interrupt."

Lauren stared at Jack. What was he doing here? Had he actually come to see her?

"I'm coming in," Jack said, "if you don't mind."

She stepped back, unsure why he was there but willing to listen. Maybe something was wrong with Ally.

After her family faded away, she closed the door behind Jack and followed him into the living room. "Do you want something to eat or drink?"

"No, thanks."

She stood there waiting, wondering why he was there.

"Can we talk?" Jack asked.

"About what?"

"About us."

Lauren stared at him. What was he talking about? "Us? What about us?"

"Well, now that my parents are moving back, I'm going to have the occasional baby-sitter, so I thought— Hell, I've been without a woman for three years. My resistance is low. When I kiss you, I have all kinds of thoughts. So I—"

"Are you asking me to offer my services?" she asked, outraged. "Maybe you've gotten me confused with the ladies we visited last night!"

"No! Damn it, that didn't come out right. I can't— Here, this will explain it!" He pulled her into his arms and kissed her. And he was right. That kiss explained a lot. It told her that he wanted her…as she wanted him. When their lips touched, they shared a wealth of attraction that they'd both been fighting.

He released her and stepped back, breathing deeply. "Do you understand?"

"I understand physical attraction, Jack, but that doesn't mean I'm going to jump into bed with you. You want the sex without sharing anything else. Certainly not Ally."

"Why should I? I'm asking for a couple of hours a week. You can spare that much time, but not enough for Ally."

"Since when are you in charge of my calendar? I make the decisions for what I do with my time. Not you."

"I don't see why this has to be so complicated," Jack said in frustration. "You feel the same way I do. I can feel it, taste it. You don't pull away when I kiss you. Are you telling me that's enough for you? Just the occasional kiss?"

Lauren turned her back on him, wrapping her arms around her body. "No, I'm not saying that. But, Jack, you're offering physical satisfaction. That doesn't last long. To not share our lives would make it hollow."

He put his arms around her, pulling her back against him. "I think we need to take baby steps. Maybe after a few weeks, we'd find the sex isn't enough and we'd move to another level. Or it could be that the sex isn't what we thought it would be and we'd drift apart." He bent down and kissed her neck, a soft caress that increased her tension.

"I don't think—"

"Don't think, Lauren. Just feel." He turned her around for another soul-searching kiss. He pulled her down to the sofa and his hands roamed her body as his kiss grew in intensity.

She could feel herself sinking into the desire he stirred in her. That desire was too powerful to resist, and she surrendered to the temptation to stroke his body. She slid her hands inside his shirt and felt the mass of muscles, the strength of him.

His hand slid under her sweater, caressing her skin, heating it up. Before she knew what was happening, he had removed the sweater she'd worn with her slacks that evening.

His lips replaced his hands as he tasted every uncovered inch of her. When his hands went to the clasp of her bra, she told herself to protest, to stop what was happening, but she was too tempted. His touch felt so good.

Before long, they were both naked and rushing toward fulfillment. When Jack stopped to put on protection, Lauren had second thoughts and considered calling a halt to their lovemaking, but then he touched her again and she was lost.

Together they reached a climax and spiraled down again.

She lay in his arms, feeling loved and cared for. A feeling she hadn't ever experienced before. She had suspected Jack was the one, but she hadn't been sure until now.

She was in love with him.

And the realization scared her witless.

After a few minutes of lying there, Jack leaned over and kissed her. Then he stood and began to dress. "Sorry to have to hurry, but I told Mom I'd be back early."

Suddenly, Lauren was conscious of her nudity and drew her clothes over her body. She didn't feel quite so loved anymore. She got up from the couch and went to her bedroom for a robe. When she came out, properly covered, Jack was waiting for her.

She walked him to the door, not speaking, not revealing her disappointment. He kissed her one more time, then simply disappeared into the darkness.

Lauren closed the door, knowing she'd just made a big mistake.

JACK FELT GREAT the next morning. Making love to Lauren had filled a void he'd had for three years. She was a wonderful lover and he looked forward to being with her again and again.

Over breakfast, fixed by his mother, he and his father talked about Jack rebuilding his construction business with his father's help. Since Jim had taught Jack most of what he knew, he figured his father would be perfect for the job of second in command. "You're sure you want to do this, Dad?"

"Yes, I'd like it. Retirement isn't for me. I don't play golf that well."

"I know of some prime property that's still available. I'll call about it this morning before I go to work. Lauren won't mind if I'm a little late. Mom, I think Ally can go to school tomorrow, but keep her down today. She likes to watch television."

"Yes, dear. And I agree. If she doesn't run any fever today, that will be two days in a row."

"Yeah. Almost three. She only ran a fever in the morning on Saturday. Are you okay with that, baby?"

"Yes, but I'd like to go to Lolly's house."

"No, you're staying here with Grandma and Grandpa. They're our guests, so be nice to them."

"Yes, Daddy," Ally said unenthusiastically.

"It won't be too hard, little one," Jim whispered. "We're easy."

Ally managed a smile for her grandfather, who was quickly becoming a favorite.

Jack went to the phone and made some calls about land and possible ventures. He was almost an hour late when he reached Lauren's apartment. But he was excited about what he intended to do. As soon as she opened the door, he announced his new plans.

Lauren congratulated him in a cool voice, and he suddenly realized she was dressed in a navy suit with a pin-striped blouse beneath it. "You going into the office?"

"Yes. I need to do some work on Robin's case." She was almost out the door as she said those words.

Jack pulled her back against him and kissed

her. She didn't seem as interested as she had last night.

Maybe she wasn't a morning person, he guessed. "Okay. I'll see you later."

Without a word, she left the apartment.

He found a pot of coffee ready on the kitchen cabinet with a mug sitting beside it and poured himself a cup. He saw his sandwich for lunch wrapped in the refrigerator. Lauren hadn't forgotten a thing. After surveying the office, he set to work. If he worked an extra hour this evening, he might be able to finish the job tomorrow. He'd planned on finishing early this week anyway. That would free him up for his new plans.

As hard as he worked, he still had time to think about making love with Lauren again. He was beginning to realize once a week wouldn't be enough. Maybe he could talk her into twice a week. Even occasionally three times a week.

It might be more difficult when he wasn't working in her apartment. When he got his new company up and running, time would be more precious. Like a lawyer.

"No!" he exclaimed out loud. Where had that thought come from? He didn't intend to get that involved in his business. He'd still have time for Ally...and Lauren. He'd just have to manage his time better.

Because he knew he was already addicted to making love with Lauren.

LAUREN WAS MISERABLE most of the day.

While making love with Jack had been wonderful, the afterglow had faded quickly, leaving only a loneliness that she didn't like feeling. She wasn't a part of his life. He wouldn't share his daughter with her, or anything else that mattered. She'd just be available for a quick roll in the hay. Then he'd be on his way.

That wasn't what she wanted.

Could she still see Ally occasionally if she didn't have a relationship with Jack?

After having spent too long at the office, she called Jack's house. Carol answered and assured her Jack was at work.

"May I pay a short visit to Ally? I miss getting to see her."

"Of course. She'll be thrilled."

"Thank you, Carol."

Lauren hung up her phone and gathered the papers she'd found for her case. Then she hurried to her car. She wanted to get there and visit before Jack came back home.

Lauren had a lovely visit with Ally and

Jim and Carol. When Jack called around five, she asked Carol to tell him to lock the door when he left.

"He wants to know when you'll be home. He's finished your office and wants you to look at it," Carol said with a big smile.

"Tell him I'll be quite late getting home. I'll look at it when I get there. But tell him thank you."

Jim gave her a sharp look, but he didn't say anything. Carol turned back to the phone.

Lauren knelt down to Ally's level. "Sweetheart, we won't see each other as often as we have, but I'll try to find time on the weekend for us to be together, okay?" she whispered as Ally hugged her goodbye.

"Okay. I love you, Lolly," Ally returned.

"I love you, too. Bye-bye."

When she got in her car, she pulled out her

cell phone and called Reggie and Robin and offered to take them out to dinner. Then she went to a late movie she didn't want to see. She sat in the darkened theater thinking about Jack until the lights came on and she went home.

When she got there, she found Jack had cleaned the coffeepot. She stared at it, trying not to think of him. Then she walked down the hall to her study. There it was in all its glory. He had done a fabulous job with the cabinets, making them a work of art. The office was now complete, ready for occupancy.

The only problem was it shouted Jack's name.

How would she ever be able to work in there? How could she forget Jack if she was in that room? How— She gave up those thoughts because she had no answers.

When the phone rang, she answered it with her name.

"Lauren, it's Jack. Where have you been all evening?"

"Out."

He said nothing for a minute. Then he asked, "Are you all right?"

"I'm fine."

"Can I come over?"

"No, I'm tired." Silent tears were running down her face.

"Did you like the office?"

"It's beautiful."

"That means I won't be there in the morning to work. But I could take you to breakfast."

"No, thank you. I have a full day tomorrow."

"How about tomorrow evening?"

"No."

"Lauren, what's going on? Why are you acting so distant?"

"I think we made a mistake."

More silence. "You mean last night?"

"Yes."

"Lauren, we need to talk about this."

Feeling her control slipping away, she managed to get out, "I can't." Then she hung up the phone.

It rang several more times, but she refused to answer it.

Somehow, she wasn't surprised when, a few minutes later, someone knocked on her door. She didn't answer it. A couple of minutes later, she heard Jack calling her name. She still remained silent.

Finally he went away.

But he'd be back. And he'd expect an explanation. One she didn't have to give. She couldn't tell him she'd fallen in love with him and couldn't accept a sexual relationship without being a part of his life. He wasn't interested in that. He didn't want to share his daughter.

She wiped away the tears and they finally stopped falling. Crawling into bed, she didn't think she would be able to sleep, but her body took over and sought the relief it needed.

LAUREN DIDN'T EXPECT Jack to knock on her door the next morning. He had plans to put into action. Their relationship wouldn't be a priority.

So when the knocking started, she went to the door, expecting it to be one of her neighbors, or a delivery, or something equally innocent. Instead she found an angry Jack on her doorstep.

"Go away. I don't want to talk to you." She tried to close the door, but he'd put his foot inside the jamb to block her shutting him out.

"Come on, Lauren. We've got to talk. You can't just stop communicating at this point."

"Yes, I can. I don't want to be part of the plan you've developed. I want you to go away."

He managed to get in her apartment and closed the door behind him. "Lauren, tell me what's wrong and I'll fix it. We have a great thing going. There's no reason to stop now."

"Yes, there is. I want to stop. That's all you need to know."

"No, it's not. You at least owe me an explanation."

He wanted an explanation? She'd give him one.

She moved away from him, putting the sofa between them. "I didn't enjoy it, Jack." She didn't pause, merely blurted, "I want you to leave, and not come back. That's what I want." It was the biggest lie of her life.

But did Jack buy it?

Chapter Thirteen

Slowly Jack walked to her, behind the sofa, his eyes never leaving hers. "I don't believe you, Lauren."

Lauren stayed ahead of him. "No, don't touch me. I don't want to have any part of the agreement."

Jack tried a new tactic. He sat down on the sofa. "Okay, so let's just talk. What upset you?"

Lauren couldn't keep walking, so she sat down in the stuffed chair that matched the sofa. "I told you it would be hollow. It would have no meaning if we didn't share anything else."

"So you want me to tell you about my plans?

I tried to do that yesterday morning, but you didn't want to hear."

He had a point. But it wasn't enough. She just shook her head.

"Look, I didn't plan on our coming to an agreement that night. So I didn't allow time for pillow talk. Maybe if we try again and allow time to talk and share, it will feel different."

Lauren shook her head.

"Why not? We were great together!"

She couldn't shake her head at that remark. It was true. They had been great together, until he said thanks and walked out. He might as well have left a twenty on the counter.

"I don't see making love as a physical workout," she finally said. "It has to have more meaning than that."

Jack frowned. "I think we'll become more to each other than sexual partners."

"No. If we start out like that, that's all we'll be. I can't do that."

With a frustrated growl, Jack stood. "Fine. My work here is done. I hope it met your satisfaction." His tone said he didn't care what she thought.

"Yes, it's lovely, thank you."

"All right. Here's my bill." He pulled a slip of paper from his pocket.

She got her checkbook and wrote him a check. Handing it to him, she started to say nice things about his work, but he walked out before she could.

It surprised her that she still had tears to shed, but she did. After an hour of crying, with nothing but puffy eyes and a headache to show for it, she cleaned up and dressed to go to the gym. There was a morning aerobics class she wanted to try.

After that workout, she came home and forced herself to set up her office. The more things she moved in, the less she remembered Jack in the room. It was becoming her office, not the room that Jack built.

She spent the rest of the afternoon working on Robin's case. Not surprisingly she found she worked better at home than at the office.

If she continued to work well at home, she might cut down on her hours at the office. Instead of working twelve-hour days, she might be able to work eight, which would allow her a life.

She immediately thought of Ally. But Jack wasn't going to let her spend much time with his daughter. She'd have to sneak some time on Saturdays.

The phone rang and she answered.

"Lauren, it's Carol Mason. Ally and I are

going shopping this Saturday and Ally asked if you could come."

"I'd love to come, Carol, as long as Jack doesn't object."

"Why would he?"

"We—we had an argument this morning. I don't think he's going to want me spending time with Ally."

"Hmm. He seems to be old-fashioned. He thinks he wants a wife who will stay home all day. I've tried to tell him— Oh, never mind. We just won't mention that you're going with us. Shall we meet at the mall?"

"Fine," Lauren replied. "And, Carol, I appreciate being invited."

"Ally and I wouldn't want it any other way."

AFTER SATURDAY'S marathon shopping trip, Carol insisted Lauren come back to Jack's·

house for dinner. "I've got Jim cooking hamburgers on the grill. I think Jack is going out this evening, so he won't be there. Please join us?"

"I don't want to be any trouble, Carol. I'm not sure Jack—"

"He told us to feel free to invite our friends. Jim likes you a lot. We'll all enjoy a quiet evening together, right, Ally?"

"Please, Lolly? I only got to see you once this week."

"All right, since Jack isn't going to be there, I would enjoy it. And we can show your grandpa all the wonderful things you bought, Ally. You're going to be the most fashionable girl at school. How is school by the way? You went back on Tuesday, didn't you?"

"Yes, but Grandma picks me up at noon and I eat lunch at home and then take my nap."

"That's terrific, honey. I'm sure Daddy is happy about it."

"I don't know. He doesn't have much time for me anymore."

"He doesn't?" Lauren asked in surprise.

"No, he and Grandpa are always talking business and writing things down."

"I'm sure things will slow down after a little while."

When they reached Jack's home, Jim did have burgers on the grill. Carol began cutting up tomatoes and lettuce. Lauren, with Ally's help, opened two sacks of chips and made some *queso* for dip.

Jim took a scoop when he entered the kitchen. "This is great, Lauren. Is it another of your special recipes?"

"No, Jim. It's Campbell's."

"I like it, too," Ally said.

Lauren laughed and grabbed a napkin to wipe the girl's face. "I can tell." But her laughter quickly faded when she heard a familiar deep voice from the doorway.

"Mom, I hope you have extra burgers. I've brought a friend."

Seeing her son, Carol showed honest surprise, almost dropping the tomato she was slicing. "Oh, yes, of course, there's extra hamburgers. Hello," she added to the woman standing beside Jack. "I'm Carol Mason, Jack's mother."

"Mom, this is Alicia Wilson. My father, Jim Mason, my daughter, Ally, and…" He looked at Lauren, but she averted her eyes. "And Lauren McNabb."

Lauren smiled at the woman, but felt awkward. Jack had obviously moved on.

As Jack and Alicia moved outside by the

grill, Lauren whispered to Carol, "I think I should leave."

"You'll do no such thing. You are our guest."

"But, Carol—"

"Absolutely not. I won't hear of it."

Ally took Lauren's hand. "Come fix me some of that cheese stuff on my plate, Lolly."

"All right, sweetie." She took Ally's hand and moved out onto the patio since Carol had nothing else for her to do. She fixed a plate with dip and chips for Ally.

"How was your shopping trip, Ally?" Jack asked.

"We bought lots, Daddy. I can show you!" She jumped off her chair to run to her bedroom.

"Not now, honey," Jack said hurriedly. "We'll look after we eat. Grandpa said the hamburgers are almost ready."

Ally obeyed, but she'd lost her enthusiasm.

"Are you her nanny?" Alicia asked Lauren.

"No, I'm just a friend."

"Oh, what do you do for a living?"

"I'm an attorney."

Alicia laughed. "You're kidding, aren't you?"

Lauren remained calm. "No, what do you do for a living?"

"I'm a school teacher."

"How nice. What grade do you teach?"

"I teach sixth grade. It's the most challenging year. The students are learning advanced math and they are learning to write essays. It's a great age group to teach." Then she looked back at Lauren. "I shouldn't have asked if you were teasing, but no one claims to be a lawyer. Because of all those lawyer jokes, I mean."

Lauren smiled briefly and passed the dip.

"Oh, Mrs. Mason, this dip is wonderful," Alicia said.

"Tell Lauren. She made it."

"Really? I can't cook anything. I mean, after teaching all day, which takes so much out of you, I just can't be bothered to cook. In fact, I usually go straight to bed for a couple of hours. Then I find something to eat, either in the fridge or I go out and pick up something. Then I have to start on my lesson plans. They're very strict about lesson plans these days."

"But I'm sure you enjoy children," Jack said.

She waved a hand. "Oh, no, I've had enough of kids. I have some neighbors who have children and they think I like to visit with their kids, and I tell them no way. I've been with kids all day long. I certainly don't want to spend my evenings with them. Except for your cute little girl, Jack," Alicia hurriedly added. "What did you say your name is?" she asked the child.

"Ally," she replied.

"Oh, yes, of course, Amy is one of my favorite names!" Alicia gushed. "I have two students named Amy. It's so confusing. I tell them every day one of them needs to change her name. But so far they haven't done so."

"Burgers are done," Jim hurriedly announced as Alicia paused to take a breath.

"I'll bring the buns," Carol said.

Since the condiments were already on the picnic table, Lauren didn't move. She was tempted to laugh at Jack's expression. He was looking at Alicia as if she were a monster. Not, apparently, what he had in mind when he'd started the evening.

"Where did you and Jack meet, Alicia?" Lauren asked.

"He's a good friend of my neighbor. Not the ones with the kids. No, my neighbor is a single guy. He went to school with Jack and suggested we might have a lot in common. And we do! We both like movies and football. I learned to love football because all the guys love football. I don't like to read, like Jack, but I don't think that matters. We have a lot of other things in common."

"How nice." Lauren took her plate from Carol and helped Ally with her plate. "Let's go sit at the table, Ally. It's easier there."

"Okay. Daddy, do you want to come?"

"Uh, I—I need to stay with my guest."

"Lolly is my guest." Ally beamed at Lauren.

Lauren got Ally a cold can of soda, then they sat at the table. She realized that, since Alicia was eating, this moment she hadn't been talking. Good fortune didn't last long.

"Jack, can you open my drink for me? I just had my nails done and I don't want to mess them up. I get them done every Saturday morning so they'll look good all weekend. And I get my hair done, too. It pays to have it done professionally, you know. These women who try to do their hair and nails themselves just don't understand."

"It's nice that you make enough to be able to afford it," Lauren said.

"Maybe if you saved a little more you can afford it, too. I know some lawyers make a lot of money but not all of you do. If you got your hair and nails done regularly, you could charge more money. I always believe you pay for what you get. So I always look good. And you know, I even won two tickets to the Cowboys football game because I looked so good."

"I thought they drew your name for those tickets." Jack stared at her.

"Well, that's what they had to say, but the

man winked at me and tried to get me to take him with me," Alicia said with a giggle. "I knew what was going on. But I'd already promised a friend he could go with me. We had a fabulous time, and we got invited to a party afterward."

Lauren took a bite of her burger to avoid having to speak. It seemed everyone had the same idea. Except Ally.

She looked at her daddy. "I won a stuffed animal at the fair once."

"Yes, but that doesn't count," Alicia said. "Now, when I went to the fair, they tried to sign me up for a *Playboy* spread, but I had to turn them down because I could lose my job, which is really unfair. I mean, how many sixth graders read *Playboy?* They wouldn't even know. They told me if I ever quit teaching, they'd be glad to photograph me."

Lauren was afraid her burger wasn't going to last long, at this rate.

"Do you ever go to the bars on Greenville? They love me there, too. I'm getting Jack to take me there after we eat. They offer me free beers if I want to dance on the bar. I always do, 'cause I love free beers. Jack won't have to pay but for three or four beers for me. If I didn't dance on the bar, he'd have to buy me a dozen."

Jim looked at her. "You drink a lot, do you?"

"Oh, yes, on the weekends. During the week, I only drink if I go to a bar to get a burger. Then I limit myself to a couple of beers. But come Friday night, I load 'em up. Once, when I was dancing on a bar, my principal came in." She giggled, covering her mouth with her fingers. "He told me I shouldn't do that, but I told him I could if it was outside school hours. After all, I do my job all week long, no matter what those kids say," she said with a bitter turn in her voice. "I shouldn't have to sacrifice my life for them!"

"So you don't really enjoy teaching?" Carol asked, looking confused.

"No. It's so limiting. I only got my certificate so I could have the summers off. Summers are wonderful. But the fall always comes. I hate that!"

"But you said you loved teaching," Carol said.

"I just say that because it's what people expect. I would guess Lauren doesn't like being a lawyer."

"Yes, I do."

"Oh. Well, you've got to be the only one. Who would like being a lawyer when everyone hates them."

"That's not true, Alicia," Jack said.

"Oh, how do you know? You're only a car-penter!" Alicia said with a laugh. "You need to get in the big leagues before you get to have a vote."

"I think Jack has been in the big leagues a lot more than you, Alicia," Lauren said.

"Yes, he has," Carol agreed.

"Well, we'll see if he parties like there's no tomorrow. That's the real test for my dates. At least, that and what happens when we get home." She sent Jack a sexy smile.

"What happens then, Daddy?" Ally asked.

Jack, Carol, Jim and Lauren supplied various answers that did not include what Alicia meant. She attempted to explain to Ally exactly what she had in mind, but Jack stopped her with a stern "Alicia!"

Lauren couldn't bear to stay any longer. She put down her hamburger, took a drink and rose. "I have to go now, Carol, but thank you for inviting me for dinner. And I enjoyed shopping with you and Ally." She bent down and hugged Ally's neck and gave her a kiss. "I'll see you soon, honey."

After she stood, she told Jim, Jack and Alicia goodbye and scooted out the door before Carol could think of anything to say.

She was almost to her car when Jack called her name. She turned around but she didn't retrace her steps. "Yes?"

"I didn't know Alicia was such a disaster. And I certainly didn't know her opinion of lawyers."

"Jack, it doesn't matter. A lot of people don't like lawyers."

"Until they need one."

Lauren shrugged her shoulders.

"Look, I don't like how we left things. Anytime you want to talk—"

"I think you're going to have enough talking this evening, Jack."

"You don't think I'm going to— I don't care what she says, I'm not sleeping with her."

"Why not, Jack? She's attractive, and she doesn't care about sharing. It's a freebie, Jack, just what you wanted."

"That's not what I wanted! I didn't mean it to come out that way, Lauren! Damn it!" He grabbed her shoulders and pulled her into his arms, his lips covering hers. When he finally lifted his head, she buried her face in his shoulder, not wanting to face him after she cooperated so thoroughly in that kiss.

"That's what made me ask. I can't explain what we have. Hell, I can't even name what we have. But it's special, Lauren. Surely you realize that."

She pushed out of his embrace, trying to

keep her face averted. "I haven't changed my mind, Jack."

He took her chin with his fingers and forced her to look at him. "That may be true, but you sure kiss like you have."

"I can't help that, Jack. Just go dance on the bar tonight and enjoy yourself."

"Right."

Lauren turned, opened her car door and got inside. She didn't want to drive away until Jack went back in the house, but he kept standing there, staring at her, so she started her car and drove off through a haze of tears.

JACK HEAVED a big sigh. If he could spend the evening with Lauren, he'd be a happy guy. Instead, he had that ditzy blonde Alicia. And he had no intention of pleasing her tonight.

He made a quick call on his cell, then turned back to the house to go get Alicia.

"Jack!"

He looked up to see her standing on the front porch, glaring at him. "I don't like my dates kissing other women!"

"I can understand that, Alicia. That's why I'm going to take you home now."

"I'm a lot more fun if I have a few beers, but if you stop and buy a six-pack on the way home, I guess we can manage, unless you're going to have some."

"Alicia, you don't understand. I'm not going to share the beers, and I'm not going to share your bed. Our date is over."

"I'm offering to sleep with you for free, Jack. Don't you get it?"

"Yeah, I get it. But I've found I'm a little picky about whom I sleep with."

"You're turning me down?" Alicia asked, shocked.

"I'm afraid so."

"Then don't bother taking me home. Just call me a taxi and I'll—"

"Already taken care of."

As if on cue, the yellow cab pulled up.

Chapter Fourteen

The next week was difficult for Lauren. She went back to work, but she left the office early several of those days and worked in her office at home. Instead of disturbing her, the memories of Jack working there seemed to comfort her. When she left her office, it was as if she left behind the good memories of the past month.

She ran into Sherry once, her downstairs neighbor, who asked again about the handsome hunk.

"He finished his job. Want to see?"

"Yes, that would be great." Once she saw

the office, she was definitely impressed. "He's really good."

"Yes, he is."

As Sherry left, two of the flight attendants from the top floor came down the stairs.

"Hey, Lauren, who was that hunk we saw around here a week ago? I think he was going to your apartment."

"He was the carpenter who redid my office," Lauren said patiently.

"We'd like his number. He looks like he'd be fun to party with," one of the women, Carolyn said, looking expectantly at her.

"Sorry, I don't have it any longer. He finished the job last week."

"Oh, too bad. If you come across it, let me know."

"I will, Carolyn. I thought the new guy upstairs might interest you."

"No, he's dull. He's a scientist or something."

"Oh, too bad."

The two women passed on out the door and Sherry stood there with her hands on her hips. "Do they think they can attack every eligible man in sight?"

"They probably can," Lauren said with a sigh.

"Did you really lose his number?"

"No. But he doesn't need help finding women."

"Good for you. I'll see you later." Sherry crossed over to her apartment.

Lauren went back inside and closed the door, going straight for her office.

Robin's case was progressing well. The investigator had turned up several enemies who might have wanted George dead. He gave the information to the police, who followed up on one of the men and finally brought charges against him, dropping any intention of charging Robin.

Robin was seeing a therapist and was still staying in Reggie's apartment. Reggie said they made good roommates.

Lauren, however, was grateful she lived alone.

Especially after Sunday dinner with James and Cheryl. James questioned her about Jack throughout the meal, until Cheryl finally steered the conversation in another direction.

After they left, Lauren leaned against the closed door, thankful she lived alone. She wandered down the hall to her study and sat down behind the desk. She ran her hand along the glossy wood, enjoying her work area. After a few minutes, she decided to go to bed early. The change of returning to work had worn her out. Better to catch up on her rest before she started another week.

The next morning she still felt a little tired, but she dressed for work and drove downtown. As she passed what had been a vacant corner near downtown, she realized they had begun building something. She looked for a sign and almost drove off the road. The building was being constructed by Mason & Company. Was that the new venture Jack had talked about?

She immediately recognized the man in the hard hat. She would never forget that body. It was Jack.

Recognizing him didn't make her day better. She was distracted all morning. Finally, she left at about two and headed home, carefully driving by the project she'd passed that morning.

"I'm going to have to find another way into work," she muttered. At home, she fixed a late lunch, but she really wasn't hungry.

She hadn't tried to contact Ally or Carol

Mason since their shopping trip. It was just too hard. Particularly if she met another date Jack might bring home. She'd decided she didn't want to know.

Obviously she and Jack had different ideas about life. She buried herself in her work. Life was easier that way.

JACK'S NEW construction company was going well. He and his father worked well together. When his father was on the job, he could leave and look for future land purchases without worrying about the work going on behind him.

Having given up on dating, Jack found life easier, but he also found it more boring. His mother had found a house in his neighborhood and his father had approved, after asking Jack if he minded. He gave his approval. Their close proximity would make life better for Ally.

And he'd dedicated himself to doing better about spending time with his daughter. Secretly, he hoped Lauren would spend time with Ally, too, but so far she hadn't shown up.

Giving up any hope of a relationship with Lauren had been impossible. He was trying to let time do away with the temptation she represented. Until he got over the attraction he felt for her, the craving to touch her, he wouldn't have a chance to find someone else.

If only she'd talk to him and tell him what had gone wrong. When he kissed her, he was sure they were on the same page, eager for each other. But she denied that yearning. He couldn't understand why.

"Jack, we need you over here," Jim called, waving for him to enter the building. He did so just as he saw a car drive by that looked like

Lauren's. He spun around to look, but it was the wrong color. What was wrong with him? He should be thinking about work.

LAUREN STARED at the calendar.

She couldn't believe she was a week late. She was never late. It must be the stress of returning to work. She couldn't possibly be pregnant. They'd only had sex once and he'd used a condom.

Deciding she couldn't sit around and wait to find out, Lauren decided to stop at a drugstore on the way home and purchase a pregnancy test. She was being ridiculous, of course. But she knew she'd worry about what was going on with her body if she didn't find out. The test would be negative and she would stop worrying.

The drugstore she chose wasn't in her

neighborhood. She didn't want to run into anyone she knew.

Lauren chose the simplest, most accurate test and also bought a couple of other things so it wouldn't look like the pregnancy test was the purpose of her shopping. She clutched the sack and hurried to her car.

Driving home seemed to take a long time to Lauren. The pregnancy test was demanding her attention.

"I'm being ridiculous. I can't possibly be pregnant."

She stopped at a stop light. "What would Jack think?" It wasn't her fault. He was the one to supply the protection. But he would think it couldn't be his fault.

"I'm right. I can't possibly be pregnant. He would make sure of that."

When she reached home, she carried the

sack into her bedroom. By now she even debated the necessity of taking the test. Finally, she decided to do so just to prove her point. She couldn't possibly be pregnant.

SHE WAS PREGNANT.

Staring at the test strip, she couldn't believe the results.

She retrieved the packaging and reread every word, looking for something that would convince her the result was an error. Instead, the packaging boasted a ninety-nine per cent accuracy rate. Was it possible she was the one per cent anomaly?

Would her doctor be willing to give her a pregnancy test?

She would need to make preparations. She certainly wouldn't give her child to anyone else to raise, especially not the father.

After a worrisome night, she called her doctor's office and explained to the nurse why she'd called.

"It's certainly a possibility that the test is wrong. The doctor will be glad to check, though it would be better if you waited another week or two."

"I'd like to go ahead and be checked as soon as possible. It's going to mean a lot of changes in my life."

"Well, he can squeeze you in at nine-thirty if you can get here then."

"Yes, I'll be there." She was already dressed and only lived ten minutes from his office. She gathered her purse and briefcase and left at once.

Half an hour later, the doctor told her the test had been accurate.

"But, Dr. Grey, we used a condom!"

"Ms. McNabb, the only truly effective way to avoid pregnancy is not to have sexual relations."

"Yes, I know."

"Do you want to keep the baby?"

"Yes, definitely."

"Will the father want to talk to me?"

"No, I don't think so."

"You will tell him, won't you?"

"Yes, of course." Eventually. When she had to.

The doctor gave her a number of pamphlets and he answered any other questions she might have.

Thanking him, Lauren left his office, her mind in a whirl. She was going to have a baby. She was going to have Jack's baby. Ally's sibling.

Sitting in her car in the parking lot, she tried to make decisions. Finally, she called the office and told them she wouldn't be in that day. Then she returned home. She went into her bedroom and put on her flannel night-gown and bathrobe, then she wrapped herself in a comforter and curled up on her bed.

She was still in that position an hour later when the phone rang. Reluctantly, she answered it.

"Lauren? Are you all right?" It was James.

"Yes, I just didn't feel quite right today, so I stayed home."

"Cheryl wanted to cook dinner for you. Do you think you'll be well by the weekend?"

"Yes, of course. That's so nice of her."

"Great, I'll tell her. And you're sure you're feeling okay?"

"Yes. I'm just resting today."

"Okay, well, save Sunday night for us."

"I will."

Several times during the day her siblings called. Each one had heard that their oldest sister was taking a day off. It was an unusual occurrence that concerned them.

Lauren got up to make herself some late lunch when she remembered it. She managed to eat a little, but her hunger was easily filled. Fortunately, she didn't lose what little she ate.

Then she returned to her bed.

When the next morning rolled around, she rose and went to work. She couldn't let this surprise development disrupt her life.

At work, she talked to the one lawyer who had gone through a pregnancy and now worked part-time at the office. She didn't reveal her secret. She simply asked how working part-time was working out.

Afterward, she wondered if she could survive on part-time wages. She had saved while she'd worked so hard to build her reputation. Those savings would come in handy now, along with her share of the sale of her parents' house. From her calculations she figured she could make it part-time until the baby was three.

"Aren't you going home, Lauren?" Judge Robinson asked as he passed by her door.

"Oh, yes, I am. I was just planning my time. Besides, I needed to make up for yesterday."

"I don't want you overdoing it if you're sick."

"No, I'm definitely not sick."

"Hey, did you see that Jack has started up his construction company again?"

"Yes, I did. It appears his parents have moved back here and his father is helping him with the company."

"Oh, really? I hadn't heard that. So you're still in touch with him?"

"Not really. But his parents arrived back here before he finished my study."

"They're moving pretty quickly. They were pouring the foundation on their building yesterday when I stopped by. I wanted to wish them luck."

"I'm sure Jack appreciated it."

"Yeah. He asked about you. I told him you were home sick. He seemed concerned."

"You shouldn't have mentioned it. I'm fine."

"Good." Judge Robinson went down the hall toward his office.

Lauren stared after him. Then she gathered her things and went to her car. When she got home, she found a message from Carol Mason wanting to know if she was doing okay because Jack had heard she was sick.

Good manners demanded that she respond, so she called Jack's number, hoping Carol would answer. Instead, Jack came on the line.

"Is Carol there?" she asked.

"No. Lauren? Is that you?"

"Yes. Carol called me today and I was returning her call." She didn't want Jack to think she was pursuing him.

"Mom and Dad are over at their new house planning where they'll put the furniture when it arrives. She'll be back soon. Shall I ask her to call you?"

"Yes, please." She was prepared to hang up but he stopped her.

"Lauren, the judge said you were sick."

"I just didn't feel well yesterday. I'm fine."

"You sure? If you need anything, just let me know."

"No, I'm fine." She hung up the phone before she burst into tears. She didn't know where they had come from, but the tears were filling her eyes.

She composed herself and went to the kitchen.

She needed to have a healthy dinner since she hadn't eaten much lunch. A few minutes later, she'd prepared some vegetables and steak.

Forcing herself to eat a good meal, she finally got up and cleaned up the kitchen. Then she turned on the television to watch a show she had occasionally watched, but it didn't hold her interest long. She fell asleep and woke up when the phone rang. She reached for the receiver.

"Lauren, it's Carol. How are you feeling?"

"I'm fine, Carol, but it's nice of you to call."

"Did you go to work today?"

"Yes, I did."

"Well, I hope you ate a good dinner when you got home."

"I did. I'm doing fine."

"All right. I just worry about you since you don't have parents to check on you."

"That's very sweet of you, Carol, but my siblings checked on me when they found I didn't go to work yesterday."

"Oh, good. Do you need to see a doctor?"

"No, I don't. I'm fine."

"Call me if there's anything I can do."

"No, but give Ally my love."

"I will. She misses you."

"Maybe I can see her this next weekend. Do you think I could take her to a movie?"

"I'm sure we can work that out. I'll give you a call on Friday evening and we'll work out the details."

"Thank you, Carol."

"WHAT DID SHE SAY?" Jack asked.

"She said she was well. And she wants to take Ally to the movies next Saturday," Carol added, throwing a challenging look at her son.

Ally cheered and immediately turned to her father. "Can I, Daddy? I haven't seen Lolly in a long time."

"I think we can work that out, baby, if you're a good girl."

"I'm always a good girl. Lolly says so."

Jack hugged his little girl. "I know she does."

"Thank you, Daddy, for letting me go."

"Yeah. I need to run some errands anyway. I can do that while you're at the movies."

"Couldn't you come, too?" Ally asked.

"I don't think so, baby. Lauren didn't ask me."

"I could ask her."

"No, you go ahead and have fun." He wasn't sure Lauren would want to have him.

LAUREN WAS SURPRISED how easily their movie date occurred. Carol brought Ally to Lauren's apartment and then she loaded Ally in her car and they drove to the movie they'd chosen to see.

"Popcorn?" Ally asked.

"Absolutely." She ordered drinks for them, too, and then they went into the theater and found their seats. They were a little early and Ally said, "Daddy wanted to come, too, but he said he couldn't 'cause you didn't invite him."

"I didn't think he'd like this movie."

"Next time can he come?"

"I don't think so, Ally. Daddy and I don't get along very well. I think it had better just be you and me." After a moment, she asked, "Did your dad not want you to come?"

"No, he said I could if I was good. And I told him you always say I'm good."

"Of course I do. That's nice of your dad."

"Yeah."

The previews began and Lauren and Ally fell silent to watch the film.

Two hours later, the lights came on and they stood to leave the theater. "That was a good film, wasn't it, Ally?"

"I loved it. Can we see it again?"

"I promised I'd bring you back home now. If we stayed to see it again, we'd get you home late. Daddy wouldn't like that."

"We could call him," Ally suggested.

"No, baby, today we'll have to get you home on time, but maybe next Saturday we can do something together again, if your daddy doesn't mind."

"Shopping! We can go shopping!"

"That's a good idea. When is your birthday?"

"I don't know. I'll ask Daddy."

"Good. If it's soon, we can go shopping for your birthday present."

"I like that!"

"I'm glad. Now, let's get you home so Daddy will let us get together again next Saturday."

"Will you ask Daddy today, Lolly?"

Lauren forced herself to swallow, when she wanted to lose her lunch. "Uh, no, not today. I'll talk to your grandmother later and work out the details. Okay?"

"But if you asked him today, then we'd know we could go shopping."

"I'm sure he'll agree. Is your grandma going to be there today?" Somehow she hadn't thought about running into Jack.

"I think so."

"Did Daddy go to run errands?"

"He said he was."

"Okay, he probably won't be home yet."

Ally didn't say anything and Lauren tried to relax. She was finding her stomach to be problematic. The thought of facing Jack this afternoon made her stomach churn.

According to the pamphlets, some women spent the first three months nauseated. Lauren was working on controlling that possibility. As long as she stayed away from Jack.

When she reached his home, she helped Ally out of the car and walked to the front door, praying Carol would answer her knock.

The door opened and there stood Jack.

Lauren looked at him and threw up.

Chapter Fifteen

"Ally, go get Grandma," Jack said quickly as he reached for Lauren, sliding his arms around her waist and giving her support.

"No!" Lauren tried to pull out of his hold.

"Relax, Lauren. I'm trying to help you."

"What's the matter, Jack?" Carol asked as she arrived at the door.

"Lauren just threw up. Can you talk her into coming in and having something to drink to settle her stomach? I think she may have the flu that's going around."

"Is that what's wrong, Lauren?" Carol asked.

Lauren managed to nod her head slightly.

She didn't dare shake it very much, or she'd throw up again.

"Then come sit down, Lauren. I'll get you some iced tea. That will help soothe your stomach. You'll feel better in a minute."

With Jack's arms still around her, Lauren managed to do as Carol asked, but all she could think about was getting away. She didn't want to confess the real reason for vomiting. Not now.

"Here, dear, sit down at the table." Carol rushed to the refrigerator and poured a glass of tea.

Lauren took a sip. "I'm fine now, Jack. You can turn me loose."

"I'm afraid you might get sick again," he said.

She could hear the caring in his voice, but that didn't mean he loved her. He was just being kind.

"No, I won't."

"I think Lauren might feel a little more relaxed if you turned her loose, Jack," Carol said. She gave her son a steady look, and he withdrew his arms, sitting back a little.

"Thank you," Lauren muttered. She took another sip of tea and then looked at Carol. "Thank you for the tea, Carol, and I'm sorry I messed up your front porch."

"It's not a problem, dear. Jim is cleaning it off. How are you feeling?"

"I think I'm okay now. I'll just leave. Thanks again."

Jack stepped to her side. "I'll take you to your car, just to be sure you don't get sick again."

"No! No, I'll be fine by myself."

"Jack, you have to let her go on her own."

"But, Mom—"

"No, Jack."

Lauren didn't know why Carol was on her side, but she was grateful. Smiling at her, Lauren slipped from the room. Outside, she paused to thank Jim for cleaning up the porch.

"It wasn't a problem. How are you feeling?"

"I'm doing fine now. I drank some cold tea."

"Glad that helped. You'd better stay down tomorrow."

"Yes, I will." She hurried to her car, determined to get away from Jack's attention.

"MOM, WHAT WERE you trying to tell me?" Jack asked after the door closed behind Lauren.

"I think you were contributing to her illness. I think she didn't want to see you."

"Why?"

"I don't know. But you are affecting her. It's up to you to figure out why."

"She won't even talk to me. I've asked her why she won't see me and at least explain what I've done to upset her."

"I don't know, son. I think she's a wonderful young lady and you should try to talk to her again."

"Should I go tonight, when she's not feeling well?"

"Maybe wait until tomorrow. I'll make something for her to eat and you can take it over to her."

Jack knew he'd be writing his script all night.

LAUREN RETURNED to her bedroom and wrapped herself in the comforter. She fell asleep for a little while, waking up around six. She thought about fixing some dinner, but she decided she just wasn't in the mood for a meal at the moment.

She closed her eyes and thought about her baby. Would she have a girl or a boy?

A picture of Jack filled her mind and her stomach started churning again. She began drawing deep breaths and blowing the air out to calm down, trying to focus on when she would know the sex of her child.

Could she ask Carol to see photos of Jack as a baby? Certainly not until she told everyone she was pregnant. If she was having a girl, she could ask to see pictures of Ally. Then she'd know what her baby would look like.

And she'd know how to decorate the nursery. She pictured a room done in pink, soft and feminine. Or blue, with a football and a stuffed bear.

Again she fell asleep and didn't wake up until morning.

JACK WAITED UNTIL his mother and Ally had gone to bed before he talked to his dad. He needed some male advice. He explained that he and Lauren had made love and it had been incredible.

"But I didn't think that would justify choosing her to be Ally's mother, because of the long hours she works."

"Did you tell her that?"

"No, I figured it would upset her. So I just suggested we…make love occasionally since it was so satisfying to both of us."

Jim's eyes widened. "Son, women are not like men. That's not a reason for most of them to have sex with you."

"But, Dad, I didn't know— Well, anyway, it didn't work out. And I tried to find someone else, but you saw that disaster. It made me realize no one could replace Lauren. But she won't explain to me what I did wrong. So how can I make it right?"

Jim cleared his throat. "What you did wrong was leave out the important words of love and commitment. And I think you can trust Lauren to be a great mother for Ally. It may not be in a traditional way, but I don't think Ally will suffer."

"No, I don't, either. You think that's all I need to do? Just tell her I love her and want to marry her?"

"If she cares for you, that should do it. And your mother will be happy. She definitely wants you to have more children."

"I don't know that Lauren will want more children. She has her work. I've accepted that. I don't want her to have a child and be unhappy about it."

"I agree, but you probably need to get her to talk to you first. Then worry about the future."

"Yeah. Thanks for helping me out, Dad. I thought maybe we could work our way up to marriage, but I'm anxious to get there however it works."

"Your mother and I want the same thing. Will this house be big enough for the three of you?"

"Yeah. I may have to build her another office here, but I can do that in my spare time."

"So you think she'll sell the apartment?"

"It only makes sense since I have four bedrooms here. But like you said, we'll let the future take care of itself."

"Yeah. Start with telling her you love her."

"I'll do that, Dad. And I hope it does the trick."

Jim went to bed and Jack wandered into the kitchen. He wasn't hungry. He was just restless. Imagining Lauren cooking in his kitchen, a satisfied smile covered his face. He would be a lucky man. He'd tried to reach happiness by working his way up to it. But he'd proven to himself that Lauren was the only one who could make him happy. The only option for him was honesty. He loved Lauren…and always would.

Tomorrow, he'd know his fate.

IT WAS LATE MORNING when a knock on her door woke Lauren up. She put on her robe and went to the door. Peeking through the peephole, she almost fell over when she saw Jack standing outside her door.

"Lauren? Mom sent you some lunch."

"Jack, I can't let you in. I'm not dressed."

"Go put some clothes on. I'll wait."

Lauren stood frozen, unable to think.

"Come on, Lauren. This soup is getting cold."

She ran for her bedroom. Searching for something to put on, something easy to slip on, she found a warm-up suit. When she was dressed, she realized she'd just done what Jack had asked without thinking.

She walked back to the door and looked out at him again. But he wasn't there. She hurriedly unlocked the door only to find him leaning against the brick to the side of the door.

"Good job. That looks great, Lauren."

She reached out for the container. "Thank you for bringing the food."

"Nope," he said, drawing his hands back. "I promised Mom I would bring it in and serve it to you."

"No, I can—"

"No," he said again and pushed his way into the apartment. He continued to the kitchen.

Lauren finally shut the door and followed him.

He had taken down a bowl and emptied the soup into it. Then he'd put the bowl in the microwave. "Sit down. It'll all be ready in a minute."

She sat down, tightly holding her hands together so he wouldn't see her shaking. He took the soup out of the microwave when it buzzed and set it in front of her. It looked like chicken noodle soup.

"It smells good."

"It is. Mom made it from scratch."

"That's very sweet of her."

"Yeah. Go ahead and eat." He put a sleeve of crackers on the table beside the bowl. "Mom didn't think these would upset your stomach."

"No, I'm sure they won't." She picked up the spoon and tasted the soup. "It's wonderful," she murmured and continued to eat. She figured the faster she ate, the sooner Jack would be gone. She was too tempted to cry on his shoulder and ask him to love her.

When she finished the soup, she looked at Jack. "Be sure to thank your mother for me. It was wonderful."

"Good. How's your stomach this morning?"

"Fine."

"You don't think you're going to throw up?"

"No."

"Well, then, it's time we talk."

"No. I don't want to talk."

"Okay, I'll talk, you listen."

Like a child, Lauren covered her ears with her hands. "No. Just go away!"

"Honey, I can't do that. I screwed up last time because I didn't explain everything the right way. Now I've got to try to straighten things out." He put his hands on hers. "Please let me do that."

She took her hands down, but clenched them tightly in front of her. Not saying anything, she stared at her hands.

"You know how I feel about Ally's potential mother."

Lauren tried to get up and leave the room, but he grabbed her hands to hold her in place.

"No, let me finish," he pleaded.

She stopped fighting him. He was going to say she wasn't right for the job, no matter what she did.

"Ally claimed you at once. And it scared me. Lawyers are prone to working long hours. My mom was a stay-at-home mom. I wanted that for Ally, but I knew you couldn't do that. Then I kissed you and—and—"

She tried to pull her hands away from him. He held them tightly, not letting her get away.

"The more I kissed you, the more I knew we were destined for each other. But I didn't think I should ask you to marry me. Not yet. That's when I came up with that silly idea."

"Which one?" she muttered, anger in her voice.

"The one where we would make love once a week."

"You made me feel like a prostitute!"

"Honey, I never meant that. I thought we could ease into a relationship. We could gradually move into each other's lives."

He lifted her hands to his lips. Then he confessed, "I knew it was a mistake right away because I couldn't wait a week to see you again. Only when I did, you were cold, dismissive. I didn't understand what I'd done that was so terrible. You seemed to enjoy our lovemaking and—"

This time she did get her hands free and jumped to her feet. She couldn't discuss their lovemaking at all.

She got as far as her bedroom door when he caught her by her shoulders.

"I'm going to throw up!" she exclaimed and made it to the bathroom.

Jack's arms went around her and he supported her while she emptied her stomach.

"Mom's going to be so disappointed that you couldn't keep down the soup."

Lauren washed her face and then buried it in a nearby towel. Finally, she said, "It's your fault, not the soup's."

"Come lie down on the bed."

"I want you to go away. My stomach will settle once you're gone."

"No, I need to talk to you. You know I tried to find someone else. I was so eager to have sex, I thought anyone would do. But I learned differently. Even if Alicia had been decent, she couldn't have replaced you. No one could replace you."

She stared at him, her eyes wide. What was he saying? And why didn't he just say what he meant? Was he going to ask her to quit her job? Should she give in to that? No, she couldn't. She'd worked too hard to become a lawyer.

Instead of continuing to speak, he bent over and kissed her, a deep consuming kiss.

She almost succumbed to his seduction, but she wrenched her mouth away. "No!"

He stayed close. "What's wrong, sweetheart?"

"You didn't finish explaining."

"Oh, right. Sorry, I got distracted." He grinned at her, but she didn't smile back. She was waiting for his demands.

"Well, see, I finally realized that you were the one for me, just as Ally had figured out you were the one for her. So, I'm asking you to marry me. I love you."

He waited, as if to hear her answer.

"And?"

"And what? Did I leave something out?"

"I'm still a lawyer."

"Yeah, I know. I'm still a contractor. Is that okay with you?"

"Yes, of course, but is my being a lawyer okay with you?"

"Absolutely. I love you. I trust you to do what is best for all of us. We both will contribute to our family's well-being. We can hire a housekeeper, if you want, so you won't have to do the cooking and taking care of Ally. We'll work things out."

She stared at him. "You're not asking me to give up my job?"

"Of course not. You're a brilliant lawyer. That would be terrible."

"But you said Ally needed a full-time mom."

"Yeah, but I bet if you asked Ally, she would say all she needs is you."

"What about other children?" Like the one she was carrying. But she didn't tell him about the baby. She couldn't. Not yet.

"I don't know," Jack said. "We'll talk about it. If you'd rather not have any babies, I can accept that. They demand a lot of time and attention."

"Wait a minute. You're willing to marry me, as a part-time mom to Ally and have no other children?"

"Yeah, if that's what you want."

"Why?"

"I told you, Lauren. I love you. We belong together." He tightened his arms around her. "You haven't answered my question. Will you marry me? And Ally?"

"Yes," she said with a sigh. "I'll marry you and Ally."

Fortunately, they were already in her bedroom. Jack made love to her in a leisurely fashion that soon evolved into a firestorm. The heat consumed her, and she forgot she had something to tell him.

JACK WOKE after a couple of hours. Making love to Lauren had been so intense, they'd fallen asleep afterward, locked in each other's arms. Next to him Lauren didn't show any signs of waking, even when he got out of bed.

He dressed and went into the kitchen to put on a pot of coffee. Then he sat down to make some lists.

Things were going to change, and he wanted to be prepared.

There was a knock on the door and he found Bill there.

"Hi, Jack. What are you doing here?"

"Lauren and I needed to talk."

"Where is she?" Bill asked, looking around. "You didn't knock her out, did you?"

"No, she's taking a nap. She's been a little off her feed lately, throwing up."

"Lauren? I don't ever remember her throwing up."

Lauren entered the room, wearing a floor-length robe. "What good would it have been if you knew? You wouldn't know what to do to help me."

"Maybe you should've stayed in bed," Bill said, not looking Lauren in the eye.

"Shall we tell him?" Jack asked her.

"He won't be able to keep it to himself," she warned.

"Honey, I want everyone to know." He smiled at her.

"All right. Bill, Jack and I are getting married."

"Well, I guess that explains the robe," Bill said in relief. "I thought I was going to have to fight Jack."

"No, little brother. I wouldn't ask that of you."

"I'm glad, 'cause I think he could take me."

Jack grinned. "I'm glad, too. I've never had brothers before. You'll have to help me get things right."

"Sure. Now you've got four brothers, counting Steve. Who you haven't met yet. He joined the army. He's away at officer's training school."

"I'll need to write him a letter, then." He hugged Lauren to him. "I think Mom will be fixing a celebratory dinner. Why don't you call all the family and have them meet us there at seven."

"Jack, you can't do that to your mother. She won't be planning on all of us descending on her."

"Yeah, she will. I'll call her in a minute to prove it." He picked up the phone and called his mother. The conversation didn't consist of much. "Yeah. I told them seven. There will be five more."

When he hung up the phone, he told Lauren, "Mom and Dad are thrilled. They haven't told Ally anything. You and I get to do that this afternoon. And she's planning on your brothers and sisters for dinner."

Lauren started blinking rapidly, trying to stop the tears that seemed to appear a lot lately. "That's wonderful," she managed to say.

Jack moved to her side and wrapped his arms around her. "Are you okay with all of that?"

She nodded, her face buried against his neck.

"What's wrong, honey?" he whispered.

"It's—it's just so nice of Carol."

"She told you she always wanted more children. I suspect she's going to adopt all your family." He kissed her, a kiss cut short by the sound of Bill clearing his throat.

"Uh, yeah, Bill?" Jack asked.

"I was afraid you'd forgotten about me."

"Not a chance."

Bill stepped back. "Maybe I'll just go call everyone about dinner."

Lauren smiled at her brother. "That'd be fine. Meanwhile I'd better go take a shower and get dressed," she said, looking at Jack for approval.

"Sure. I'll go home and see if I can help Mom. I'll come back for you at six-thirty. Okay?" When she nodded, he bent to kiss her again. "Mmm, I'd better get out of here before I lose control," he said with a big smile.

When he left, Bill stared at Lauren. "Are you happy, sis?"

"Oh, yes. I didn't think I could be this happy. He doesn't mind that I'm a lawyer."

Bill looked confused. "Well, of course not. You're a great lawyer."

"Yes, but I'm also going to be a mommy. For Ally," she added quickly, lest Bill catch on to her secret. She realized then she still hadn't told Jack.

"Yeah, but you'll do that well. You were a

great mom for us. I remember when I figured out you were only a year older than me. I couldn't believe it, but you always acted like you were lots older."

She gave Bill a wobbly smile. "I hope I can do as well with Ally."

He came across the room and hugged her. "You'll do fine. Jack seems to think so. Now go get showered. You have an engagement party to go to."

Chapter Sixteen

At dinner that evening, with Jack's dining table expanded to hold all his guests, Ginny wanted to know when the wedding would be.

"As soon as possible," Jack said. "Lauren, do you want a huge wedding?"

She shook her head. "No, I'd like a small church wedding with my family and yours."

"Good. How soon can we do that, Mom?"

"Well, we'll have to find a church, and of course a dress."

"I'm making the dress," Reggie said. "I can have it ready in a week."

Lauren smiled at her sister. "That would be lovely. Something simple."

Ginny added, "I'll check with my minister. Our church is small, so it's not as well-booked as the big churches."

"Oh, good. And we'll need a florist," Carol said, ticking off a list she suddenly pulled out of a pocket.

"I've got a buddy who owes me. He's a florist," Barry said.

"Wonderful. We'll need a cake." She looked around the table.

"The restaurant where I waitress makes beautiful cakes." Ginny gave a big smile.

"Well, this is getting easier and easier." Carol turned to Jack. "You'll need to get rings."

Bill knew a jeweler who would give them a

good deal and fit the rings immediately. And Carol told them she would cater the reception.

"So how about next weekend?" Jack asked Lauren softly.

"I think we'd better make it the weekend after that, to give Reggie a little time."

"Okay, but it's going to be hard traveling back and forth."

"Back and forth?"

"From your place to mine. We are going to live here, aren't we? I mean, I have four bedrooms, and you only have three, and one of them is a study."

Lauren stared at him, reality hitting her in the face. "I have to give up my beautiful study?"

"The one I have here is almost as good. We'll share it."

"Please, Lolly?" Ally said, reaching out for her hand. "Please marry Daddy?"

"Oh, sweetie, of course I'll marry Daddy. I just hadn't realized I'd have to give up my study."

"But you get to be my mommy!" Ally reminded her.

"True. And that's the best part!"

Jack leaned in closer. "The *best* part?"

"Behave, Jack Mason!" Lauren warned in a whisper.

No one noticed, because they were all discussing the details of the wedding.

"Lauren, dear, you'll need to make a guest list of your friends," Carol ordered.

"But I thought we'd just have our families."

Jack grinned. "As much as I'd like that, you can't get married without Judge Robinson and his wife being invited."

"Yes, I thought he might walk me down the aisle."

"Hey, I was going to do that," Bill protested.

"Oh, how nice of you, Bill. Of course, that's what I'd like."

Barry and James were looking a little left out. "Can you guys be my best men?" Jack asked them.

"Sure," they both returned, smiling.

"Good," Lauren said. "That will balance out Reggie and Ginny. And Ally shall be my flower girl."

"I will? What do I do with the flowers?"

"You sprinkle them on the floor as you walk down the aisle," Lauren said, hugging the little girl.

"That will be fun."

Not half as much fun, Lauren thought, as marrying her handsome fiancé.

ALLY WASN'T SO SURE it was going to be fun two weeks later when she faced a church full of people.

"Mommy," she whispered to Lauren. She'd immediately started calling her Mommy when they told her they were marrying. "I think I'm afraid to go down there by myself."

"But you'll be following Reggie and Ginny. And everyone wants to see how pretty you look in your new dress." Reggie had not only made the wedding gown but also hers and Ginny's gowns and Ally's.

"Can't I wait and go with you?"

"Not this time, angel. But I'll be right behind you, with Bill."

"I like Bill."

"I'm glad. Now, there go Reggie and Ginny. It's almost your turn."

Ally, with a little more encouragement,

went down the aisle, carefully dropping one rose leaf each time she stepped. When she reached the altar, she went to her daddy, who sent her to the ladies' side.

Then it was time for the bride.

Lauren stepped into the aisle in the dress Reggie had made her, an a-line skirt with beads around a heart-shaped neckline. Bill stood proudly beside her.

They had come a long way, she and her siblings. As Jack had said, Carol had adopted all of them in her heart. Jim seemed happy with that, too.

They passed Carol and Jim, and Lauren took a rosebud from her bouquet and handed it to Carol as she continued to the altar.

When the pastor asked who gave Lauren to this man in marriage, to her surprise, all her siblings said together, "We do."

Lauren blinked, trying not to cry, as Jack took her hand from Bill. He squeezed her hand to encourage her.

She suddenly regretted not telling him about the baby yet. There just never seemed to be the right moment to share such momentous news. But Jack, she realized, should've had a choice. But he'd said he loved her, and she believed him. And she loved him.

When the ceremony was ended, the pastor told Jack to kiss his bride. He did so enthusiastically before he turned her to face their guests. The number had swollen a little, until the small church was filled. It resounded now with applause for the newlyweds. The reception had been moved from Jack's house to the church hall, and Carol had had to hire some caterers to prepare the food. Jack led

Lauren to the party, and they danced their first dance to the music of a small band.

"You realize we've never danced together before?" he murmured in her ear.

"There are a lot of things we've never done together," Lauren said.

"True, but we'll get around to them. We've got a lifetime together to try everything."

She looked up into his eyes then, aglow from the hundreds of twinkling lights that lent a magical feel to the church hall. In those eyes she saw the love he felt for her, love she returned in kind. And that's when she knew this was the right moment she'd been waiting for. "We're going to raise a child together," she told him.

"I know. Ally is so excited to finally have a mommy."

"No, I don't mean Ally."

"What are you talking about?"

"I should've told you earlier. Then, if you didn't want a baby, we—"

He came to a stop. "Are you telling me you're pregnant?"

She nodded her head. "That's why I was so sick." She smiled tentatively. "I'm so happy about it. But you never said anything about a child. The longer I waited to tell you, the more afraid I became. So I didn't tell you. I hope you're happy."

He said nothing. He just picked her up and spun her around, holding her close.

"Careful, my stomach isn't too strong," she said laughing.

"Did I remember to tell you I love you?" he asked when he put her down.

"Yes."

"Well, I love you even more for wanting to

have our baby. Ally will have a brother or a sister! Wait until she finds out."

"Wait until your mother finds out," Lauren murmured. She knew Carol wanted more grandchildren.

Jack laughed out loud. "Oh, mercy, she's going to go crazy. You'll have to be strong about what you want and don't want, because she'll get carried away." He kissed her.

"Now, I have to go dance with my mother and you'll dance with my father. We'll share our news with them, okay?"

"Are you sure this is a good time?"

"It's the best time, sweetheart. Go," he said, pushing her toward his father after another kiss.

Lauren asked his father to dance with her, and he immediately put his arm around her and danced her away. "Are you okay? You looked a little stressed out there. Is Jack behaving himself?"

"Yes. I had to give him some news, and I thought I should've done it before the wedding."

"What news was that?"

"I'm expecting a baby in eight months, Jim."

"Oh, my, that's wonderful news. I'm going to be a grandpa again. Have you told Ally yet?"

"No, I thought I should tell Jack first."

"Yes, of course."

Across the room, they heard Carol scream. Jim said, "I think she just got the news. Here they come."

Jack and Carol reached them and Carol wrapped her arms around Lauren. "Oh, I'm so happy! It's going to be wonderful."

"I'm glad you feel that way, Carol. I felt bad not telling you sooner."

"Well, I understand that you had to tell Jack first. But I think it's wonderful."

"Me, too," Jim said, shaking his son's hand.

"Oh, my, our family is growing by leaps and bounds. Now when we get your brothers and sisters married, I'll have grandchildren everywhere!"

"Let's take it one at a time, Mom. I'm going to be nervous going through the pregnancy thing with Lauren. I want everything to go well."

Lauren took his hand and carried it to her lips. "It will go well, Jack. I'm sure of it."

EIGHT MONTHS LATER, Lauren gave birth to her son, Robert James Mason, named after his grandfather.

Ally stared at the baby in her mother's arms. "Is he real?" she asked.

"Yes, he'll wake up in a minute and let you know he's real. He can scream louder than you, sweetie."

"Why?"

"Because that's how he lets us know he wants something."

"What does he want?"

"Usually a dry diaper and a bottle, in that order."

Ally watched in fascination as Bobby preceded to do exactly as his mama had promised.

"Daddy, is he going to live with us?"

"Do you want him to live alone, baby?"

After a moment, Ally said, "I guess not. He's my brother, but we need to teach him to talk so he won't scream."

Jack was changing his diaper. "I agree, and there are a few other things he'll need to learn, but he's got a big family to teach him, starting with you."

"Me? I'm going to school now to learn things. He'll have to go to school, too."

"Yes, he will," Lauren agreed. "But you'll have to teach him to speak his first words, and take his first step."

"Boy, it's not easy being a big sister, is it?" Ally asked.

"No, but it's a great job!" Jack said as he handed the baby back to his wife with a kiss.

* * * * *